A Change of Pace

Shelly Lawson

Dedication

Dedicated to all those avid readers out there and to all those that helped make this book happen.

Chapter One

"If all three of you get knocked out simultaneously, I may have to leave you for dead." Thus was my warning as my oldest three brothers struggled with my huge suitcases, their knees buckling at each step as they make their way toward the front door of our house.

"That wouldn't even be a danger if you hadn't packed an entire drugstore's worth of makeup," remarked Dillon, one of my younger brothers.

"Yeah, well, we can't all be as secure with our looks as you are. Anyway, my makeup happens to be in *that* bag," I mentioned matter-of-factly as I pointed at one of the bags that Marshall had swung over his shoulder.

Suddenly, all progress stops short as my mother appears, holding a tray of lemonade and cookies, resulting in the box I was carrying running smack into one of their behinds. Exasperated by the new box-shaped pit in my abdomen, I let out a deep groan.

"Sorry, sis, but I've been smelling those cookies and they just smell too good to pass up. Not to mention, she cut me off of dipping into the raw dough a while back."

"And, if I hadn't, you wouldn't be enjoying the product of the baking process *now*, would you?" my mother quipped back.

"On a side note, Sam, I'd be extra careful back there behind Nick. The term 'silent but deadly' was coined with him in mind. Heck, when he was little, he practically didn't even need a stroller; he could just propel himself around with the power of methane." Dillon pointed at his slightly shorter twin whose back I had run into.

I was about to remind him that I had ringside seats to that gaseous period when our brainy little sister Jillian walked in and interjected.

"Actually, the term 'silent but deadly' was widely used in the 1950s which, as you know, was decades before Nicolas was born."

"We know, Jilly. It was a joke, unlike our dear brother's stench problem." I made a face.

"Yeah, especially after the three bean-and-cheese tacos he inhaled for lunch." Marshall threw one of the mammoth-sized bags by the door and plopped onto the couch. Suddenly, a shrill scream came from the top of the stairs:

"Mommy!"

Growing up, the Palmer household was rarely quiet. With seven children, our parents never had a chance for a quiet life. Marshall, who was destined to be a soccer player from the very start of life, was first to grace my parents with his presence. When he hit his 'terrible twos,' anything and everything that wasn't nailed down was fair game, and was promptly kicked over and/or stomped on as if it looked better that way, after which he would just stand there and grin as if he had achieved a great accomplishment. Needless to say, my parents could not wait until he grew out of this phase. It was about this time that I came along. I was the completion of that perfectly even family of a mother and father with one boy and one girl that graced the front of magazines at every supermarket. At this point, our family was very satisfied with the way life was. For quite a while it was just the four of us living comfortably on our 8-acre piece of farmland. Once I got a little older, Marshall and I would spend hours exploring the property and imagining up things like turning an old septic tank we found in the bushes one day into a torpedo from WWII or a rusty old yellow truck bed perched on top of four 55-gallon drums into a two-story bungalow.

It was when I was six years old that my parents were blessed with another baby girl: Colleen Rae Palmer, weighing in at 6 pounds, 13 ounces. And, even at nineteen, she doesn't weigh much more than that, having been blessed with a great figure and the ability to maintain it no matter what she ate, much to the annoyance of every girl she came in contact with throughout the years. Colleen was a typical girl from the very beginning. From an early age, she developed an interest in Barbies and play makeup, which consequently covered the floor of the bedroom we shared, much to my annoyance. And, unlike our much younger sister, Marshall and I had been taught early on in life to keep our toys picked up, so when I stepped on Malibu Barbie's pink pump on the way to the bathroom in the middle of the night, I knew who to throw it at.

Two short years after Colleen was born came the twins, Nicholas and Dillon. By this time, my parents had grown fond of the idea of a big family, and decided to add onto the house in preparation for even more children.

They had no idea what they were up against with those two as the boys are constantly up to something, especially now, at the age of seventeen. Not to mention, the scrapes and bruises that those two alone accumulated had us going through Band-Aids like they were Skittles. It's even a running joke in our family. Any time someone visited, whether for dinner or the weekend, the hostess gift was always the same: Sport Band-Aids.

A few years later, my dad was in a terrible accident that put him in the hospital for about a month followed by a year of intensive physical therapy. My parents were afraid they might not get to have the Brady Bunch family they had imagined. Then, one day a few years later, after a routine checkup at the family doctor, my mother was shocked with the news of little Jilllian's impending arrival. My parents were so overjoyed, they held a block party that will be remembered for years to come.

Of all of our family, Jillian has got to be the most unique. She was blessed with brains AND brawn. She's the type that could be reading Jane Austen with one hand while hog-tying the dog with the other. Fifty percent of her time is spent with her nose in a book, studying some subject that would give a college graduate a run for their money, and the other half out training Mr. Darcy, her most prized family member. I don't know what made my parents buy a horse, but I also wasn't dumb enough to look a gift horse in the mouth. (Pardon the pun).

Though my parents were quite aged by this time, their final production came as no surprise to anyone: Baby Brian. Brian is significantly younger than the rest of us, so he revels in being passed around by the whole family and completely spoiled by all. An inside joke of our family is that there will be a huge parade at every major AND minor event of his life, from his first potty to his funeral. And that sweet little boy is where the afore-mentioned holler came from. Unfortunately for my little brother, the oven timer for the cookies that my mom was baking had gone off at the same instant. Being that I was the only other person standing at the time, I was elected as the obvious choice to go and investigate. I didn't mind, though, because I knew that my time with my baby brother was quickly fleeting, being that I was leaving in a few days. You see, I was going to be staying with my aunt and uncle in New York for a while and I didn't know how long I was going to be staying, so, naturally I relished the idea of spending a private moment with little Brian while I was still around.

I bounded up the stairs to my little brother's room. It was supposed to be his naptime, so I had a suspicion that he had had a bad dream. When I entered his room and saw that he was sitting up in his bed, eyes red and watery, my heart leaped out to him.

"What's the matter, Bri-Bri?" I asked, as I snuggled under the covers beside him on his little twin bed.

He crawled in my lap, raising his hands above his head, saying,"I dreamed that New York ate all of your socks and you had nothing to wear on your feet to go running!"

"Really!" I said, squeezing him tight and urging him to go on. This seemed like one of those moments where you just want to pause time and stay in forever.

"Then a monster came along and you couldn't run because you didn't have socks and it ate you!" I looked down at my little brother and smiled.

"Well, you know what? I heard about those sock-eating monsters."

"Really?" he asked with a sniff, his eyes as big as saucers.

"I sure did. Then I went out and bought a whole bunch of extra socks, so you don't have to worry about any trouble with them." I assured him, in as serious a tone as I could muster.

"Whew, that's a relief!" he said, making a theatrical gesture of wiping his forehead.

I seized the opportunity, now that his arms were out, to give him a little tickle. He giggled and wrapped his little arms around me so tight, I thought I might cry from how wonderful this moment was. "You know what?" I said, "I think I might miss your big bear hugs most of all."

After savoring the warm, fuzzy moment for a few more seconds, the smell of a fresh batch of cookies wafted in from the kitchen, resulting in a convulsive jarring from his squirming little body as he struggled with the covers. Once he was uncovered, all that was left was a little blur as he made his way toward the tantalizing treats. I stared headlong into the doorway of the little bedroom for a few moments longer before I crawled out of the tiny bed and made for the door myself.

After such a touching moment, I couldn't help but think about how difficult it was going to be to leave my home and this loving, warm environment. But, as much as I loved growing up with a big family and care for each of them dearly, I had felt that it was time for something different, something new and exciting. I just wasn't sure what. I had spent countless hours throughout the past few weeks trying to think of something I could do to get away from the norm for a while. I had tried to come up with ideas before, and on many occasions could not come up with a single one. So, I would just start doodling and getting further away from my original purpose. Then, last week, after I had spent about half an hour in my room, wracking my brain, Marshall knocked on my bedroom door, came in and plopped on my bed.

"So, how's the brainstorming coming?"

"Pretty confusing."

"Maybe I can help." Marshall and I had always had a very close relationship. On some occasions, it almost seemed like we were reading each other's minds. So, he had always been the first person I went to when something was bothering me, and tried his best to be there for me every time he could be. So, considering that I was going to be asking him for help eventually, I happily accepted his help. As soon as we got comfortable, I told him all about how I was feeling bored and needing to get away from the norm for a while, and he listened and understood.

A short time later, my mom came in with the phone, saying it was for me. "Well, who is it?" I asked, my brows furrowed with curiosity. "It's your Aunt Beth. She wants to talk to you about something." Elizabeth Calame, or Beth as she is more affectionately known, is one of my favorite aunts. She and her husband, Uncle Joe, live way up in Hillsdale, New York, a small town on the northern side of the state.

With a confused look on my face, I took the phone. Within seconds, Marshall had hopped off the bed and taken his leave along with our mother to give me some privacy.

"Hello?"

"Hi, honey, it's your Aunt Beth.

"Hi! What's going on? How are Janine and Kim?" My uncle and aunt have two daughters, Janine and Kim, who are both very successful businesswomen in the city.

"Oh, I suppose they're doing okay." she sighed. After a few moments, she went on. "Ever since they moved into that new apartment in the Upper East Side, I haven't heard from them very often. I guess that means they are enjoying themselves and their newfound independent state. And your uncle Joe has been working on some new highly-classified, super-secret project, leaving me to entertain myself most of the time, so I thought it might be nice to have someone come up and keep me company for a while. Would you like to come hang out with your old auntie?"

"Oh, Beth, that's an awesome idea! That sounds like just what I need! Just give me a little while to talk to my parents. I will try to call you later tonight. And, by the way, you are far from old."

"Oh, how sweet! I knew I picked the right niece! Anyway, that sounds great, sweetheart. Look forward to hearing from you. I love you, and give my love to the rest of the family."

"I will definitely do that. Bye." As soon as I'd hung up the phone, I got up and ran to the family room to tell my parents about my aunt's invitation. But, of course, they already knew. I guess Beth had already asked their permission before talking to me. The rest of the afternoon was spent with half of the family, going around and around, trying to come up with a plan that suited everyone's needs. Finally, there was a consensus: Since Marshall was the type of protective older brother that did not want his little sister getting lonely,(or at least, that was the explanation he came up with; but knowing him better, I knew that he was just looking for a break from work), he willingly offered to accompany me, to ensure my safety. Then, after a brief discussion with our parents, it was decided that we would take the old family station wagon with us. The station wagon had been the family vehicle for a long time until about a year ago when my parents decided to buy an upgrade. The ensuing argument between all of the kids that were of the driving age (and even some that were not) in the house made my parents decide that it would sit in the driveway until someone absolutely needed it.

I would say that this definitely qualifies.

Chapter Two

One Week Later

Though we had traveled up here about once every few years for my whole life, I'm never quite prepared for the amazing beauty of the area my aunt and uncle live in. Their house is situated on a small hill right across the street from the beautiful Lake Copake. It was really like a scene from a movie or a painting. The grass was as green as could be and every yard was peppered with tall trees, which lended a warm feel and were very well-manicured.

Across the skinny gravel road, there were trees with their branches making artistic shapes of dark wood contrasting with their backdrop of sky and lake that seemed to come together as they mirrored one another, coming as one in an ethereal illusion. Across from each cabin was a small dock for each resident to park their kayaks. Plus, every few slots, there was an even bigger dock for those who were rich enough to have speedboats.

The cabin where Aunt Beth and Uncle Joe lived was a cozy little three-bedroom house of a sort of maroon color with old wood everywhere that reminded me of what I had imagined everyone's house was like in the old days. Yes, this was definitely exactly what I needed. I had a feeling this was going to be really great. I sighed with hopeful excitement as I pictured outdoor barbecues, lying on the hammock whiling the day away with a good book, paddling a kayak on the lake and so many other wonderful possibilities.

"Well, I don't have to guess at what a hernia feels like now," Marshall complains as he hauls one of our suitcases over to the area of Janine's old room. "Do you, by chance, have a large rock collection I don't know about?"

"If I did, I'm far too old to have such an attachment to it that I'd bring it all the way from Texas to New York."

"I'm not here to judge. Where do you want it?"

"Oh, just set it inside Janine's old bedroom. When Beth gets in, we can figure out sleeping arrangements. I'm not sure if she's expecting other guests or not."

"Sure...Um, what are you doing?" he asked as he came back into the living room from tossing the bags in our cousin's old room and leaned against the corner of the wall.

Sitting on the wood floor, I clutched my foot. "I think these bags are out to get me. They've been trying to fall on my toes all day. Well, they can bust out the maracas now, because they finally succeeded."

"I tried to tell you not to bring all your makeup in one bag." Despite my totally-done-with-your-jokes-right-now glare, he looked away and smirked at his own cleverness. I continued to cradle my foot.

"Well, you are just a stitch today, aren't you? Owww, speaking of stitches..." I said, as a sharp pain hit like a strike of lightning. "Don't help at all, though. I'm just trying to wait for it to stop throbbing, then I'll go out behind the shed and rub some dirt on it." Taking the hint, he came over and crouched beside me tentatively to take a look at my now purple-and-black toe. He grimaced. "Wow, you really did a number on it, didn't you? You have any idea where Aunt Beth has the antiseptic stashed?"

"Not a clue. Somewhere in the bathroom, I would guess." Due to the fact that I was in pain, my reply came out a little more catty than I meant it to be.

As if on cue, the door slides back open as my ever beautiful and effervescent aunt appears. "Hello, my loves! Sorry about my tardiness. I was out in the back shed, seeing to your uncle's lunch. He'd be a real work machine if it weren't for that *eating* habit he seems to be so fond of. So glad to see you both... Oh, dear, did you hurt yourself? Here, let me go get you something for that." Then, as quickly as she had appeared, she was gone. We heard shifting and tinkering going on for a few seconds, then we watched as she reappeared with a little white spray can. I cringed at the very sight of it.

"Oh, don't be a baby. You girls were always the biggest wimps growing up. Suck it up and take it like a man," Marshall taunted, still kneeling in front of me.

"We girls were wimps because you boys were always up to something mischievous, and we were always on edge, just waiting for whatever it was, and yet it still caught us off guard every time." I expressed mock horror at the fact that this diversion even made my aunt chuckle.

"Sit back, son," ordered Aunt Beth. "If this stuff gets in your eyes, you'll feel like your uncle did after his brief attempt at beekeeping."

He laughed and obediently crawled a few feet backwards. As the cold spray hits my foot and begins to sting, I let out a groan. He chuckles again. "Aww, come on, it can't be that bad."

"Oh, really? Come over here and say that." I held out my pinchers, which made him curl his legs under his chin. I lay back on the floor and tried to think of something more pleasant.

Grinning at me, then looking at her watch, Beth says, "Well, you're all patched up, here. What do you say we take a break and get a bite to eat?"

◆ ◆ ◆

"So, do you have a specific place in mind, or are we just going to wander around until we either find something or starve?" I stared out the window as we drove through the small town of Hillsdale in search of food.

"I know *just* the thing! Have you kids ever had bagels?"

"Yeah, Mom buys them at Walmart for us all the time," Marshall declared from the backseat.

This made Aunt Beth chuckle. "No, no, no, no. Those aren't *real* bagels. You haven't had a bagel until you've had a real New York-style bagel, fresh from the oven." There was a strong sense of pride in her inflection.

"Hmmm, I guess I had just figured they were all the same," I reflected.

"Oh, honey, there is nothing like a bagel from New York. And *pizza.* Before you leave here, you must have a slice, or I haven't done my job as your hostess." After saying this, she veered into a space at a quaint little place that screamed home-cooking. It was sort of like a little corner bistro, with little striped canopies over the windows and tables which had umbrellas over them, where you'd imagine freshly-manicured women-of-leisure sat to people-watch, observing the huddled masses of New Yorkers with something or other to do, rushing from place to place as if their feet were on fire.

So, we got out, locked up the car and collapsed at the first available table, despite the strange looks coming from every direction. It felt strange to be practically on display, like some diorama in a museum or something. It seemed like every single person in the area stopped to gape at the obvious out-of-towners

To our relief, the waitress came right up to us, and gave us our menus. I looked up to see a five-foot-three redhead with twinkling blue eyes. She was wearing a pretty true-blue button-down dress and some moderate navy slingbacks. Her hair was pulled back loosely into a beautiful little turquoise butterfly clip with gems in the marcasite settings, and a bunch of mountain curls flowed down her back like a babbling brook over river rocks. I was amazed that *anyone,* much less someone who spent as much time on their feet as a waitress could still look good at this time in the afternoon, but this girl looked as though she'd just stepped out of the salon or on the cover of one of the chic fashion magazines that are sold at practically every street corner. I looked over at Marshall and I could swear, any second, that his jaw was going to start rubbing against the sidewalk. His eyes were as big as sand dollars. She set the menus on the table in front of us and said, "Hi, Beth! Welcome back! What'll you have? The usual?" At my aunt's nod, she turned to us, saying, "And I don't believe I've met your company. Hi, I'm Catherine Myer, but my friends call me Cat." She extended a perfect hand to each of us. Aunt Beth took it upon herself to initiate the introductions.

"This is my niece Samantha and my nephew Marshall. They came all the way from Texas to spend some time with their old auntie." She gave us a proud, affectionate wink.

"Oh, wow! Me too! I mean, I'm not visiting, but I moved here from Texas myself."

Just then, another waitress approached, saying, "Hey, Cat, can you cover my tables for a minute? These heels are killing me and I haven't gotten to pee in three hours."

"Sure thing, Paige," she said to the fellow waitress then returned her attention to us. "When you guys know what you want, just holler at me." She shook our hands once again before walking over to clear the dirty dishes off of a neighboring table.

I leaned in to whisper to Marshall. "She's gone now. Will you close your mouth before you drool all over the table?" I couldn't help but chuckle.

"Ha ha, you are hilarious," he replied indignantly.

"C'mon, it's okay if you like her. She's cute. You should go for it."

"Keep your voice down. She'll hear you. Anyways, I don't know where you women get these idiotic ideas. Why does every woman have this pathological need to fix every single person you know up with a date without even laying the proper groundwork, such as, I don't know, *actually speaking verbally to her?* Besides, she's way too pretty to go out with a simple guy from Texas like me."

"Hello. Did you not hear her say she is also from Texas?"

"That's exactly my point. She's from there but she didn't *stay* there.

"And?"

"And she obviously had her reasons for leaving. Plus, we won't even be here for more than a couple of months and what then?"

"Okay, okay. Calm down. You're worse than us girls. Why don't we look at our menus now?"

After a few moments of silence, he said "Everything sounds so good."

"Well, hurry up and decide what you want to eat before we starve. Plus, the sooner we decide, the sooner she'll come over," I said, smiling at the picture of my brother picking up chicks at a diner.

Once we'd made up our minds, I gestured to Catherine to let her know that we were ready to order. She sauntered over and gave us her best Hollywood smile, pulled her order pad and a pen with a fluffy feather topper out of a little pouch in her apron, and waited for us to tell her what we wanted.

Like a true professional, I thought.

◆ ◆ ◆

When our gigantic, meal-sized bagel dishes came, we were completely delighted to find that they were not at all like the rubbery refrigerated ones that we were used to, but were actually quite a pleasing experience. The outside was beautiful and glossy while the inside was baked to perfection and the taste was like nothing we had ever had eaten before. We ate in complete and utter silence, savoring each bite thoroughly.

When we had finally decided that we could not possibly eat another bite of our food, Catherine reappeared and, rather efficiently, began to clear the table. She then offered to box up the remainder for us to take home. Once she had done so, she asked, "May I ask where in Texas y'all are from?"

I noted the use of the Southern colloquialism "y'all" and was about to reply when, to my surprise, Marshall actually spoke.

"Near San Antonio," he said. I was proud of him for taking the step to talk to her without his voice cracking. I gave him a slight nod of approval then turned my attention back to Catherine.

"Wow, that's a *long* trip. How long are you going to be staying in New York?"

"Actually, we aren't sure. We're just sort of playing it by ear. Marshall runs a moving truck company back home, so he is going to have to get back to it eventually. But, other than that, nothing is pressing."

"Well, the reason I ask is because our best busgirl is pregnant and is taking her maternity leave in about a month, so we need someone to fill her shoes in that time. Normally, it would be up to the manager to fill the position but she's my cousin, and has a bit of a Napoleon complex and delegated it to me so she could spend more time with her annoying boyfriend. Anyway, she feels very rushed, and has decided the position needs to be filled in the next few weeks, so I'm basically asking anyone I see that has half a brain. So, if you do decide on an extended stay, it could provide you with a little more spending money while you enjoy the sights on your visit. Who knows, it might even make you want to stay for an extended time."

I decided to go for a noncommittal approach. "Oh, I'm really not sure how long we are staying but I can call you and let you know once I find out." *How strange,* I thought, *approaching total strangers and giving them a job! I don't know about this...*

"Okay, sounds great! I'll let my boss know you might be interested!" She began to turn away.

"Oh, Cat darling," Aunt Beth interjected, with a wink directed at Marshall. "You know, these two deserve to get the best look at this fine area while they are here, and my knees aren't cooperating well these days, so I thought perhaps on one of your days off, you could help me out by showing them around."

"Sure, I'd be happy to oblige. Hey, you know, I have tomorrow afternoon off. Why don't we get together then?"

"That would be great! We are up for anything. This is a vacation, after all. We'll probably still have a bit of unpacking to do in the morning and then we can meet you here for lunch and go from there." I was getting excited about this.

She pulled out her order pad and fluffy pen once more, jotted something down, tore it out and handed it to me. "This is my mobile. I pretty much answer it every time when I'm not working. It kind of freaks people out because sometimes I answer on the first ring. It always catches people off-guard. It's like they aren't quite ready to talk yet. You know, like when people use the time when the phone is still ringing to gather their thoughts. Well, anyway, you have my number. I've got to get back to work now, but I will see you tomorrow. Bye." With that, she turns away and saunters over to another table and two waiting customers.

◆　◆　◆

"I'm *serious,* Marshall. Didn't you think it was rather odd that she would just hire somebody literally right off the street?" I asked as we sat on our twin beds after having finished unpacking already. We weren't sure which room we were going to end up with because my aunt tended to have one or more of their friends or even just some of the local homeless population spending the night, but since no one was in there at the time, we chose the twin room. Beth was well-known in the area for this generosity; Some call it quaint; others, naïve, but we just call it her 'Bethness'.

"I don't know, sis. It might not be such an uncommon thing in this area. Plus, she seemed like a perfectly innocent girl, especially if Aunt Beth likes her."

"Maybe you're right. I guess I'll just have to get acclimated to things around here." Then, after a few seconds, I chuckled. "You sure are in a hurry to defend this girl..."

"Ugh not this again. Goodnight, Samantha." He got under the covers of his bed and rolled to face the wall.

Then, suddenly feeling like a nine-year-old again, I continued to taunt: "Oh, *somebody's* defensive. This must be worse than I *thought. It* must be because you *looooooove* her!"

"Okay, whatever you say. I'll propose first thing tomorrow. Do you have a ring I can use?"

His frustrated sarcasm was very satisfying to me. On that note, I decided to crawl into my tiny bed and turn in. However, about the time I was beginning to fall asleep, I was startled when Marshall leapt out of his bed. I nearly jumped out of my skin. "I almost *forgot!* I got you something on the way up here." He trotted across the room to the dresser.

"Jeez, you scared me half to death!" I clamored to reach the switch for the bedside lamp.

"Sorry. I just happened to remember. Anyway, I saw this in a store earlier and thought it was pretty cool, so I got it for you." He sat on the end of my bed and handed me a little black box.

"Marshall, I love you too but I think, if we got married it would raise some eyebrows," I teased.

"Just open it."

"Okay, okay." I flipped open the little box and inside was the strangest thing I'd ever seen. It was a ring with the face of a watch. My brother had always had the oddest tastes in toys.

"Well, what do you think? Isn't that the coolest thing you have ever seen?"

I decided to just go along with it. "Yeah, this is really cool! Where'd you find it?"

"Oh, it was in the window of one of those novelty stores we passed by on our walk with Aunt Beth in town. Oh yeah, and it's waterproof, so you don't have to worry about getting it wet."

"Thank you. This is a sweet gift." I leaned up to initiate a hug. He got up from his seated position and hugged me back. "We should get some rest."

"I'm with you on that one. See you in the morning." He got into his bed and I turned out the bedside lamp.

Chapter Three

The next morning, I woke up really early, so I decided to get out of the house to keep from waking anyone up. I got out of bed and threw on my fuzzy purple robe and matching slippers. I decided to sit on the patio for a few minutes and sip a small cup of coffee. About halfway through my coffee, I heard a strange noise. Then, out of the corner of my eye, I noticed that the door to the shed was slightly ajar, so I decided to go and investigate. I got up, tied up my robe tightly, as if this would give me any protection whatsoever, and made my way over, my curiosity piqued.

It was dark inside the little shed, so I opened the door wide, using a nearby fire log from the stack along the side of the tiny building to prop it open. I knew that Uncle Joe had a project going in here, so I decided that it would be best if I didn't uncover anything in my effort to make sure that nothing else was out of the ordinary.

"What are you up to this early in the morning?" came the voice of my uncle from inches behind me, sending shivers down my spine. Suddenly, something didn't feel right. I had to think of an explanation as to my being in here.

"Um, I thought this might be a good time to go for a kayak ride. I woke up early for some reason and decided to get out of the house because I didn't want to wake anyone up. It just looks like such a peaceful morning, doesn't it?"

Now facing him, I saw the expression in his face turn from creepy to skeptical. "In your *robe?*"

Oh, crap. How am I gonna talk myself out of this one?

"Oh, that's right. I guess my brain isn't completely present yet this morning."

"Okay, dear. You run along and get changed. Meanwhile, I'll work on getting this stubborn thing down from the rack.

I walked back to the house and tiptoed in, sliding the door as slowly as possible so as not to slam it, then snuck into the bedroom. I glanced at Marshall, who was fast asleep and didn't move a muscle, went to the closet, opened it as carefully as possible and retrieved the first clothes I saw: a turquoise bra, an orange T-shirt, some blue jean shorts and, of course, underwear. I also saw the ring-watch and decided that it might come in handy. I took the few seconds to set it by my phone and then slipped it onto my left middle finger. I took another wary glance at Marshall, who seemed dead to the world, walked to where there was a chair between him and me, just in case he were to wake up, then performed the fastest change of underwear in history, threw on my bra and the rest of my clothes and, with a sigh of relief, began to tiptoe out of the room when all of a sudden, one of the floorboards I stepped on made a deafening creak. Holding my breath, I looked back over at Marshall, who had stirred but still hadn't fully woken up. I got out of the house as fast as I could.

Once I'd gotten outside, Uncle Joe had unloaded one of the kayaks from the wall-mounted rack. "Would you mind helping me get her down to the water?" He held out the two halves of the oar to me.

"Not at all." I grabbed the handle at one end of the kayak and we made our way down to the water.

"Have a nice time. Your aunt usually has breakfast ready around eight-thirty." He started to turn back toward the top of the hill but stopped and looked at me, "And, next time you need something out of that shed, why don't you just let me know so I can take care of it for you."

A shiver ran down my spine. *What is he up to in there that he doesn't want me seeing? He is acting so strange.* I smiled, trying to seem nonchalant. "Okay, great. Thanks for the help." He waved a hand as if to say it was nothing then began to ascend the small hill toward the shed once more. I watched him for a few more seconds, then connected the two halves of my oar and used it to shove off from the bank.

When I had paddled for a short while and was out toward the middle of the lake, I stopped to take a rest and gaze at the breathtaking sunrise. I held my breath for a few seconds, willing the moment to stop right where it was as everything disappeared; No stress, strange waitresses, suspicious uncles, or any other life complications, just peace and the overwhelming feeling of how small I am as compared to the immense sky above me. I leaned back a little more to take in the warmth of the sun's rays gently warming my body. *No moment could be more perfect.* I checked my ring-watch to see that it was only six-thirty. No one else would be awake yet, and I *definitely* wasn't going to be shooting the breeze with my uncle who may or may not be into some shady business. That's the last thing I need to get sucked into. I paddled around for about half an hour longer, then decided to head in to the shore to go for a walk around the neighborhood and get back in time to make the family breakfast since I was the one who was already up.

I had gotten about a hundred and fifty feet from the shore when I noticed a group of people hanging out on the dock next to Beth and Joe's. Normally, I would just ignore them, but something inside me prodded me to paddle in their direction. As I came nearer, though, I began to make out the face of one of them who looked sort of familiar, but I was still too far out to see for sure. I squinted my eyes and slowly paddled in the direction of the group.

It couldn't be, I thought. *It's impossible. What could he possibly be doing here?* I stopped, as I realized that I was looking straight into the face of my ex-boyfriend, Jacob McAnnely.

♦ ♦ ♦

I hadn't seen Jacob since he'd proposed to me three years ago. We had met when we were nine years old when he and his foster parents who, at the time, were in the process of adopting him moved down the block from us. One day, they just dropped by the house to meet the new neighbors. I was the first to answer the door and there he was. We became fast friends. He, Marshall and I spent every minute we could playing together. Little did we know that we had found a friend for life.

Marshall sometimes teased me about Jacob's intentions, but I always shrugged it off. Then, one day when I was nineteen, I came home to find his truck parked in front of my house. Curious, I went inside to see what he had come over for. The moment I opened the door, I could tell something had changed. Then, after some stammering, her finally came right out and said it: "I've asked your father's permission to date you. I've been wanting to tell you how I've felt for so long."

I remember being so shocked and thrilled at the same time that I was lost for words for a few moments. When I could finally speak again, all I could utter was one word in acknowledgement: "Okay."

We were together for three years, and we loved each other but I was twenty-two and I felt like there was more I could do with my life before settling down and getting married. So, we parted amicably and I hadn't seen him again until now.

I began to row as quickly as I could toward my own dock, until *SPLASH!* The kayak flipped over, dumping me into the frigid water. It might have just been my imagination, but before I hit the water, I could have sworn I heard my name uttered. "Samantha?"

While submerged and trying to make sense of which way was up and which was down, I heard another splash. Thank *goodness! Marshall must have gotten up and come down to the water and seen me fall in!* So, when I was wrapped in two muscular arms that were bringing me to safety, I couldn't have been calmer. When our heads were finally above the surface of the water, I could not hold back my gratitude. I wrapped my arms around the familiar neck of my rescuer. Only, this neck was familiar in a different way than my brother's. I loosened my grip and looked at the face of my savior. Imagine my shock as I look into the face, not of my brother, but of Jacob.

"Hi," he said. Suddenly uneasy, I wriggled from his grasp, and moved toward the kayak, which was upside-down a few feet away.

"Well, thank you for saving me, but I need to get this kayak out of the water."

"Here, let me help," he offered.

"Oh no. I've got it." I was very much on the defensive.

"Don't be stubborn. That thing is gonna be full of water. *Please* let me help you."

When I gave him an icy look, he threw up his arms and backed off. "Have it your way. If I had a white flag, it'd be up in the air. I'll just hang out over here and watch then," he said in that annoying *you-couldn't-possibly-do-it-without-me* kind of way.

Trying my best to ignore his obvious attempt to get a rise out of me, I nodded my head toward his group, which, I noticed, included several thin bikini-clad women. Rolling my eyes, I scoffed, "Don't you need to get back to your *entourage?"*

"Oh, they can wait." He seemed a bit satisfied by what might have appeared to him as my jealousy. Completely annoyed, I scowled at him, then turned my full attention toward the kayak. After a few minutes of tugging and grunting, to my utter annoyance, I could not budge the kayak, so I had to accept his help. The second the kayak was grounded, though, I was *so* out of there..

"Wait," he said, grabbing my arm, not tight enough to hurt me but tight enough to where I wasn't going anywhere. When I made an attempt to break from his grasp, he let go, but whipped around in front of me. I bowed my head to keep him from seeing how badly I did not want to be here. "Please, just listen," he urged, the faintest tone of the little boy I once knew in his voice. Looking him in the eye would be a huge mistake right now, as it would reveal the little girl I had once been rearing her head, and willing my eyes to well up. I pushed the tears back, willing all the bitterness I had in my arsenal to show clearly in my eyes. Reluctantly, I met his gaze.

"That sure is a lot of hate to show the person who just saved your life," he said, holding his hands up like I had a gun pointed at him.

"Are you kidding me? I may have been a helpless little doe-eyed teenager when we were together but I've since learned to swim," I replied indignantly.

"First of all, I'd hardly call twenty-two a teenager," he began, ignoring my horrified expression, "and secondly, forgive me for feeling a responsibility as a human being to help *anyone, especially* someone I *knew* was not a strong swimmer." He sat on the bank, then turned to me with intense feeling in his face. His voice softened, as he finished his soliloquy. "Imagine my relief to know that such is no longer the case."

Needing to lighten the mood for both of our sakes, I said, "I took lessons at the community center about a year ago. Now, you need to get back to your group and I need to go put on some dry clothes."

Switching back to heroic mode, he scrambled to his feet. "Let me walk you up."

"No, please. I'll be fine. Plus, the last thing I need is Marshall passing out at seeing you here, resulting in me having to clean up a huge mess," I said with a smirk as I continued to climb the wooden steps toward the road. I hadn't realized I had hurt my ankle until I began the climb. No sooner than I had landed my foot on the first step did the pain start. When I doubled over in pain, Jacob rushed over to steady me.

"Okay, first of all, I think your very wet clothes are going to cause a mess anyway, and there is no way you're making it all the way back to the house on your own. I don't care what your brother has to say, I'm helping you." Of course, I had no way of refusing this gesture.

◆ ◆ ◆

Back at the house, everyone was already awake, sitting in the TV room and drinking coffee; Except for Uncle Joe, of course, who was reading the paper. It was worth all the stress and pain of the morning just to see the shocked expression on everyone's faces, especially Marshall's, as Jacob carried me with ease into the house and set me on the leather couch in my still-quite-wet clothes.

"What happened?" Uncle Joe asked.

"Her kayak turned over on her."

"Let me go and get some towels for both of you."

"Why did she need carrying?" Marshall probed, folding his arms and fixing Jacob with a skeptical stare.

"Well, I'm no expert of course but, I'd say she has a sprain in her right ankle. A few weeks in an Ace bandage should fix it right up. You can get them at any drugstore. Also, icing it will help the swelling."

Once they had all recovered from their momentary shock of witnessing this spectacle, they all jumped to action. While Jacob propped up my ankle on a pillow, Marshall proceeded to fill a gallon-sized bag with ice and Uncle Joe retrieved a pillow for my back from the guest room.

When all this was done, Beth volunteered to start making breakfast for everyone. Jacob declined her invitation to stay and eat with us, saying that he had some company he needed to get back to.

"Plus, judging by the twenty shades of white Marshall is turning, they are all gonna want the story on what just happened." And after one last look my way, he left.

With more concern than the rest, having been around for the breakup, Marshall came over to the couch and whispered so that the others would not be able to hear. *"Jacob? Seriously? What's he doing here?"*

"He didn't say."

"Are you going to be okay seeing him around, bumping into each other all the time while we're here?"

"I'll let you know when I find out. Now, let's hurry up and eat our breakfast," I prodded. As he helped me up, he reassured, "I just want to make sure you're alright."

"Yeah, I know," I sighed. "I just don't know yet. All I can tell you now is that it is definitely gonna take some getting used to. Now, would you be so kind as to give me a hand getting to our room so I can get out of these wet clothes." I pulled back the blanket, revealing my very wet clothing.

"Boy, you really went for a swim," he chuckled.

"Yeah, well, you know how I just love a brisk swim at sunrise," I replied.

On the way back out to the living room, my ankle gave yet again, nearly causing me to fall, had Marshall not been supporting me. "That's it," he said. "We need to call Catherine and tell her we won't be able to make it. We can just reschedule for another time."

"That might be a good idea," I agreed.

"Meanwhile, I'll see if Uncle Joe will take me into town and get your bandage. You just rest. Who knows? Tomorrow, you might feel good as new."

♦ ♦ ♦

As it turned out, Marshall had been right. The next morning, between the ice and sleeping with it elevated, my ankle *did* feel better. Again, I woke up earlier than the rest of the family. Still, I didn't want to aggravate the injury further, so I decided not to go kayaking. Instead, I made myself some coffee, fished a book I had borrowed from Jillian out of one of the bags in my room and decided to make myself comfortable on the front porch.

As soon as I got out the front door, I ran smack dab into the torso of someone who'd chosen an odd hour to visit, spilling my coffee in the process. I looked up to see that it was Jacob. As I began to lean down to pick up the now-empty cup, he held out his hand. "Please. Allow me." He bent down, picked up the cup and handed it to me. "Wow. Sorry about that. I just wanted to come by and see how you are doing." He flashed that scruffy Southern grin that still drove me wild to this day. Then, looking me up and down, he said, "It looks like you're doing pretty well actually. Glad to see you're up and kicking."

"Yeah, it does feel pretty good today. It was very thoughtful of you to think of me. I appreciate it." *Maybe this won't be as hard as I thought it might be.*

"Of course. Mind if I join you?"

"No, not at all. There's plenty of coffee in the kitchen if you want some," I said as I turned around and carried my cup back inside to refill it, leaving the door open as an invitation for him to follow..

A Change of Pace

"Sounds great," he said as he followed me into the kitchen.

"The cups are in that cabinet," I said, pointing.

"Got it," he said. At this point, all the small-talk was held off until we got back out to the porch.

"So, how weird is it that we both traveled across the country only to end up right next-door to each other?" I asked when we had settled ourselves back on the porch.

"Er, very. What are you doing in New York?"

"Oh, I just thought it might be nice to get away for a little while. It seemed like a nice idea for a bit of a change of pace, you know?" I sat back in the wicker chair, took a sip of my coffee and sighed with contentment. I felt the cool northern breeze dance around my face. I curled my toes and tucked my legs up underneath me.

We sat there talking about all the things that had happened since we'd last seen each other, keeping away from subjects like relationships and such for the next couple of hours until it was time for breakfast, after which he gracefully trotted back to the cabin next door. I sat there watching until he disappeared from sight behind the huge trees between the two properties.

Chapter Four

"Are you going to tell me what's going on between you and Jacob?" Marshall asked suddenly as we were finishing up the dishes after dinner that night.

I looked over at him, confused as to the source of this train of thought. "Well, it's actually pretty simple really: Nothing. Absolutely nothing." I tried to keep my eyes out the little window above the sink as I said this.

"Are you sure he knows that?"

"Well, yeah," I said. Then, less convinced, I added, "I mean, I think so."

"Oh, I beg to differ, little sister."

"What do you mean? Is there something I'm not catching?"

"What I mean is, isn't part of the reason you came here to forget about him?"

"It's been three years, Marshall."

"Which is nothing if you ever loved him."

"That's not fair. I do-I mean did love him."

"Ah, and there it is. I knew it was a bad sign when he showed up yesterday." His tone was rising now. "You came here for a change; Well, you're going the wrong direction, sis."

"Keep your voice down," I shushed him.

"Just," he paused, sighing, "be careful. By the way he's been looking at you, it's not over for him either and it won't be long before he makes a move and you both get hurt."

"That's not going to happen."

"Okay, as long as you think you're safe, I trust you. You're my sister and my best friend and you know I love and am completely loyal to you, but he was my friend too as you'll recall. It isn't just him you'll be hurting if things don't work out."

◆ ◆ ◆

The next morning, when Jacob came over bearing a bouquet of half a dozen sunflowers tied up with a single white ribbon, I couldn't bear it anymore. Hurting him again was the last thing I wanted, but I couldn't disappoint Marshall or my family and I couldn't hold my thoughts in any longer. Trying with all my might to keep my composure and not turn into a blubbering idiot, I made it through the greetings, then suggested we walk down to the dock.

Once we got down to our destination, he held the flowers out to me. "I can't take those," I said as carefully as possible. He looked at me as if I'd said something funny. *Perfect. He thinks I'm just being polite.*

"Nonsense. I got them for you," he said with a very cute chuckle that made me wish my heart would just shatter into a million pieces and end my misery.

With all the bravery I had in my arsenal, I raised my head to look him in the eyes, oh those wonderful eyes that looked at me as if looking at all seven wonders of the world at once. "Trust me on this one, okay?" I felt hot tears well up in my eyes. Quickly, he set the flowers on the table and walked over to console me, but I pushed him away, turning my back because I couldn't stand to see the worry in his eyes.

"What's going on, Sam?" he asked tenderly. Still looking out to-ward the lake, I gave in to the emotion, to all that I was feeling and the urgency of it all. I wept as though I would carry on forever. It was a solid ten minutes before the sobbing quieted. And Jacob's standing here with me, trying to be supportive the whole time was not helping matters.

Once the flood of tears had quieted, he nudged me as if willing me to confide in him. "You wanna tell me what this is about?"

I wiped at my tear-streaked face before I could look at him. "It's about us," I said almost inaudibly.

Lowering his face, he said, "I figured as much."

Panicking now, I continued. "You have to understand, this was not what I wanted when I came here. I came here to get *away* from the drama."

"And I guess it found you, huh?""

"You have no idea," I sighed.

Suddenly, as he was looking at me, his eyes turned cold and angry. "*I* have no idea? Are you *kidding* me? In case you've forgotten, this isn't the first time we've been in this situation. In case you didn't realize, *I'm* the one that keeps getting rejected! What's your excuse this time? I've gotta know!"

When he had finished his tirade, I stayed quiet for another few minutes. In fact, it was quite a long time before either of us spoke again.

"I never meant for this to happen again." I sighed. "It's just that I really thought we might be able to put our past behind us and be friends again, I truly did. But, then Marshall-"

"*Marshall? What* does *he* have to do with this? Now it's so clear. You don't need anyone else because you're practically *married* to your brother! Tell me something. Is there *any* decision you make for yourself?" Before I could say anything, he stopped me. "Don't answer that. Honestly, I don't think you've ever once made a single decision for yourself. You know what? Let me know when you grow up." With that, he turned his face toward the water as if he couldn't stand to look at me another second.

Not sure I could bear his scorn any longer, I began walking back toward the cabin. Once I was up beside the road, despite everything I ever knew about love and breakups telling me not to, I looked back toward the dock to see his shadow hurtling the sunflowers into the lake.

♦ ♦ ♦

Once I'd gotten into the house, I went straight to the bedroom and got into my little twin bed and screamed into my pillow.

This time Marshall jolted awake. "What? What's happening?"

I turned to face him, my head still on the pillow. "You were right."

He sat up in bed, rubbing his eyes. "I was? About what?"

"Jacob. He still loves me and I'm a terrible, terrible person."

"Wait, are you crying? What did he do? Do I have to punch him out now?"

"No, don't do that. He was right. It's my fault. I shouldn't have led him on. I'm a terrible person."

"Stop saying that. You're not a terrible person. No matter what you did, he was going to believe what he wanted to believe."

"You think so?"

"He's a man. It's what we do. Now, get up and come have some coffee with me."

I took a deep breath. "Okay,"

◆ ◆ ◆

That afternoon, we had invited Catherine to come over for some kayaking after which Uncle Joe volunteered to barbecue. We figured it was the least we could do after my injury had prevented us from visiting with her the other day. When she knocked on the sliding glass door, I answered it cheerfully and offered her some fresh lemonade.

"No, thanks," she said. "I'm on a bit of a health kick. No sugar for me. Besides, I'm ready to get out on the water if you guys are."

"Okay, well I think Marshall needs a bit more time. He volunteered to help one of the neighbors finish building his dock. It shouldn't take much longer."

"No problem. We girls can just hang out and chat until he gets back." She sat on the couch and I sat by her.

No sooner had we gotten comfortable, however, did Marshall walk in the door, soaked to the bone with sweat.

"Did you already go for a swim without us?" I laughed as he made a big production of wiping his forehead.

"Enjoy your laugh at my expense. It's boiling out there. I hope you girls put on enough sunscreen.

"I've got it right here." I patted my bag. "SPF 50. The good stuff."

"Okay then. Shall we?"

We spent the afternoon paddling around in the kayaks and enjoying a cooling swim, while Uncle Joe prepared the barbecue pit and cooked some steaks. He summoned us when the food was ready. As we ate, we all enjoyed each other's companionship, though it seemed that Marshall and Catherine did most of the talking. He seemed much more confident this time. They talked about their likes and dislikes as well as their goals. None of the rest of us could get a word in edgewise. We didn't mind though. We just ate and listened.

As the night progressed on, however, it came time for Catherine to head home. "Well, it was really nice getting to know you folks," she said with a big, happy smile.

"You too," I answered, even though I knew that it was really directed at Marshall.

"Good night." She smiled at me

♦ ♦ ♦

The next morning, Jacob did not visit. I looked through the trees toward the neighboring cabin to see that his truck was not there. I thought this was quite odd, but decided that maybe he had work to do or something. When I started back toward the porch, I noticed that Uncle Joe was already up and busy in the shed. Not wanting to disturb him, I began to tiptoe across the lawn back to the house when I heard him call out to me from the shed. "Well, now, look who's up and at 'em at the crack of dawn like always.

Recovering quite quickly, I replied, "Yeah, I've been really enjoying the mornings here."

"It's too bad your boyfriend couldn't come and visit you today." His mouth curved into a knowing smile.

"Huh? Oh Jake. No, no. He's not my boyfriend." I felt my face start to get hot with embarrassment. *Let's just nip that notion in the bud right away.*

"Oh, pardon me. I just assumed, since he's been coming all this way every morning to see you, that something was going on." *All this way?* I looked back at the fifty yards between the two cabins.

"Well, now you know."

"Yes. Now I know."

I was about to ask about the 'all this way' comment when I spotted a green truck behind the shed. I was sure I'd never seen it there before. As if sensing my knowledge of his presence, a tall, older fellow emerged from the shed.

Uncle Joe looked back toward where I was staring. "Oh, pardon me, Samantha. This is an ex-colleague of mine from the old firm. He's been helping me on a project."

"How do you do? I'm Darren Andrews."

"Nice to meet you." Then, after a few awkward seconds, I dismissed myself. "Well, I don't want to keep you from your project. If you don't mind, I have to go get ready for the day." I half-jogged back to the house to wake up Marshall. Today was the day, now that my ankle was feeling a bit better, we had made plans with Catherine to go to the city and I knew he'd want plenty of time to get ready.

After taking my shower, I threw on my robe and went to wake Marshall up.

"Good morning, sleepyhead," I sang cheerfully, to which he responded with an enormous yawn, stretching and blinking his eyes a few times.

"Well, it's morning anyway." He's not much of a morning person.

"Oh, don't be such a baby. Anyway, I figured you'd be rushing *me* out the door, considering our plans for the day." I shot him a sly smile. That did the trick. He hopped right out of bed and threw the covers up so that the bed looked somewhat like it had been made.

"I'm fairly sure I left you some hot water for the shower, but you may want to have a cup of coffee first to let the water heater build back up," I directed as I grabbed his bathrobe from the closet and tossed it to him.

Once he was taken care of, I opened my side of the closet to look for something to wear. After a brief search, I picked out my favorite black sweater and some green cargo pants, brushed my hair and tied it back, then realized that my colorblind brother would, undoubtedly, need my help in picking his wardrobe. I got dressed and started to look for something for him to wear. I looked through his side of the closet for a few minutes until I found a nice pale green pinstripe shirt that I had bought for him a month before. I looked over at the ring-watch on the nightstand and decided to put it on. Afterward, I went back to getting the wardrobe ready. I paired the shirt with some hunter-green slacks and laid it out on his bed. With that finished, I went to put on my makeup using the natural light from the bedroom window and a hand mirror I had brought from home.

When Marshall finally emerged from the bathroom, being ready myself, I grabbed my purse and went to the living room. Aunt Beth, who had just gotten up, was on her way to the kitchen.

"Good morning," I said cheerfully.

"Good morning, dear," she almost whispered as she got one of the large coffee cups out of the cupboard and poured herself some coffee. "Are you kids going to be needing some breakfast before you go?"

"Oh, that's okay. We can just grab a bagel at the diner before we head out to the city."

"Okay, that sounds perfect." Then, suddenly, her expression changed to one of discretion. "I'm surprised your gentleman friend hasn't visited today, or has he already gone?"

"Oh, Jacob? I don't know. I guess he had something to do this morning." *Is the whole town going to ask about him today?* "Not that that's a bad thing, I guess. It's no big deal. I've got better things to do than shoot the breeze anyway," I said, trying to convince *myself* more than her.

Blessedly, just then, Marshall emerged from the hallway. "Ready to go, Sam?"

I breathed a sigh of relief. "I was born ready. Let's go." I grabbed his arm and gave it a tug in the direction of the door.

"Hold it." *Oh no.*

I looked back at him, exasperated. "What now?" I practically hissed.

"Geez. Calm down. I was just gonna ask where the keys are."

"I have them in my purse." We hugged Aunt Beth and headed out the door. I noticed that Mr. Andrews' truck was still behind the shed. I really wondered what they could be working on, but I shrugged it off. I shoved the key into the ignition, gave it a turn, only to find that it wouldn't start.

I tried it once more.

Nothing...

Finally, on the third try, the engine turned over. Marshall and I looked at each other and breathed a sigh of relief.

"Guess we will all have to get used to this cooler weather up here." Marshall said, giving the dashboard a sympathetic tap. I put it in reverse and gently let up on the brake.

Suddenly, glancing over toward Jacob' s house, I gasped. It wasn't Jacob, but some other strange man lurking near the neighbor's house. I couldn't believe my eyes! I stepped on the brake, causing the car to jerk to a stop, startling Marshall.

"What is it?"

"Look over there. Do you see that?" He looked in the direction I was pointing in the neighboring yard, then back at me with a scrutinizing look.

"Yeah, sis. It's a man. I'd have figured you'd be used to them by now," he joked. I gave him a look that said "Hello...?"

"Okay. I am sure there is a perfectly normal explanation, but, just so you will feel safe and secure, I will go see what he's up to. You stay here, alright?" Ignoring his thick sarcasm, I watched as he got out of the car and proceeded to walk toward the man. As soon as Marshall called out to him, the man put on a big smile. From what I could see, he seemed pretty friendly. I suddenly felt guilty for being suspicious, so I decided to bite the bullet, put it in park, and go introduce myself. I wasn't about to turn it off, for fear it didn't start back up.

I was greeted by him with wide eyes and a bright smile when he saw me coming in his direction. The mysterious man continued the conversation.

"I completely understand you young people wanting to be more careful than was required some years ago. This is an old community. You would be pretty surprised to hear about some of the things that have gone on in this neighborhood."

"I don't believe we've met." I said, holding out my hand for a handshake. "My name is Samantha, and this is my brother, Marshall. We are staying with our aunt and uncle for a while."

"It's a pleasure to meet you both. My name is Nathaniel. Nathaniel Grey. I've been living in this neighborhood for over forty years." Motioning to his eyes, he continued, "These eyes have seen some pretty strange things in their days. Patrick, a man who lives on the other side of the lake, and I like to get together on the weekends to exchange stories while we play a little five card draw. He can't bluff to save his life, but he sure does have a lot of interesting stories to tell."

Marshall chimes in finally. "Well, we'd love to hear some of them, but we are meeting someone in town and we are late. It was very enjoyable talking to you, Mr. Grey…."

Nathaniel interrupted, saying, "Please, call me Nathaniel. Mr. Grey makes me sound so old."

"Okay, Nathaniel it is then. We've got to go for now. It was a pleasure, and I am sure we will be seeing each other around, being that we are neighbors for a while now and all."

Well, our fears allayed, we could enjoy our day with Catherine. Although we were both still worriedly observant to the sound of the engine for the majority of the 10-minute drive to Hudson, it seemed like Marshall had something on his mind, though he wouldn't say.. Then, just as we pulled up to the diner, he looked at me as if he was about to say something. I waited, wondering what he could be thinking about, but all he said was, "I am sure Catherine is waiting for us." Then, in the next second, he opened the door to the truck, got out, and slammed it *hard!*

◆ ◆ ◆

"Hey guys!" Catherine was picking up some dirty dishes from the table near the door. "Let me just take these to the guys in the back. I'll be right back." A few short seconds later, she reappeared from the kitchen. " It's about time you showed up! I was about to give you up for dead," Catherine mock scolded, hands on hips like an angry mother. And with her apron on, she looked just like Donna Reid or one of the other house-wives of old TV shows. Then she softened and joked, "By the way, don't worry if the cops bust down your door sometime today looking for you. Just tell them to call me." She almost made it through, but at the end, she was not able to keep a straight face.

"Sorry, we had a little misunderstanding to settle this morning. But, we finally got everything out of the truck. Now, all we have left to do is figure out what to do with everything," I said apologetically.

Catherine nodded understandably. "It happens. Don't worry. I am just kidding anyway. I knew you guys would show up eventually. Do you want something to eat before we head out?" She handed us a couple menus with a big smile.

"Um, I think I'll have an onion bagel with caramelized onion cream cheese spread and honey ham. What about you, sis?"

"Well, I think I'll try a blueberry with straight cream cheese, fresh fruit compote and a side of ham."

She scribbled down the orders on her little order pad and began to head back to the kitchen.

"Wait, aren't you going to eat something?" I asked.

"Trust me, my friend. When you work in a place like this day in and day out, you are eating this stuff all day." She gave her best imitation of someone who'd eaten way too much, and continued on her way.

When she came back a few minutes later with our orders, Marshall was more than happy to take his.

"Thank you", he said, biting into it with a voraciousness I had never seen before, then said, mouth (and face) full of food, "Do I have something in my teeth?" I gave him a look of mock horror, which made him laugh, spewing moist pieces of food everywhere the process, which made me laugh even harder. Marshall had always been the one to go to when I needed a laugh. As for the rest of the restaurant, however, they all grimaced at the sight.

And, of course, at this moment Catherine walked back in looking ready to go. "We'd better get a move on. We don't want to be late."

"Late for what?" I asked, curiously.

"You'll find out when we get there," she laughed. Marshall and I looked at each other and shrugged our shoulders simultaneously. (Ain't it grand how siblings can do things like that?) Then, we followed Catherine out the door of the comfy little café to our mystery destination in the Big Apple and its bustling city streets. As we set out on our journey, we had no way of knowing what could be in store. How we would navigate the convoluted maze that is the streets of the Big Apple, we knew not, but each of us were sure that an exciting adventure, and possibly an enduring friendship was ahead of us.

◆ ◆ ◆

Once we had stopped at Starbuck's and each gotten our favorite drink, we were on our way to what I had decided to call 'Catherine's Mystery Destination'. As we walked down the sidewalk, I was imagining all kinds of different scenarios where she was an international spy and she was taking us to an undisclosed location or she was a hit man, or hit woman in this case, taking us to a dark alley to whack us where no one would hear our screams. I laughed at the sudden urge to smell my venti nonfat mocha latte as if it contained arsenic.

As we rounded the next corner, I was flabbergasted to see Jacob at a nearby hot dog stand. *This city could not possibly be that small,* I thought as I took hold of Marshall's arm, praying not to be seen by Jacob. That was the last thing I needed.

Yet, to my dismay, his glistening dark brown eyes met mine before I could look away.

"Well...we meet again," he said, then turned his attention to Marshall. "Hey Marshall, long time no see," he said, as they shook hands.

"It certainly has been quite a while," Marshall replied. "We haven't gotten much time to talk since you saved Sam's ankle. What have you been up to other than heroic stunts?"

"Other than school, you mean?" Marshall nodded. "Well, I've tried a few different jobs, trying to find my niche. I just started working with a local construction company. I realize it's not a glamorous job, but it pays for the spaghetti-ohs."

"Cool. Have you gotten used to the big city life yet?" Marshall asked.

"Well, it has been quite a while. It was rough for the first couple of months, but I got used to it. It gave me a much-needed distraction at the time, you know, right after...." He suddenly turned his head down in sorrow as if to say "Well, you know."

An awkward silence set in, as all four of us, including Catherine, who had no idea what we were talking about, stared at our feet. Marshall and I, of course, knew he was referring to the day that Jacob had proposed to me.

After a long awkward silence, Marshall, suddenly aware of Catherine's presence, said, "Oh, and this is our new friend, Catherine. She's showing us around the city today."

Jacob turned his attention to her. Shaking her hand, he said, "It's a pleasure to meet you. These two haven't driven you crazy yet, huh?"

"Well, she hasn't quite known us long enough," Marshall said. "I give her a week."

Giving him a playful look, she said, "You know, just because I live in New York, doesn't mean I'm a city girl. I'm tougher than I look."

"Okay, make it two weeks," he joked as she elbowed him in the ribs good-naturedly.

"So, where are you three heading?" Jacob asked.

"Oh, we're just going to grab a bite to eat and do some exploring of the finer spots of our fair city."

Just then, I saw a man that looked exactly like the man we had met this morning, only much more mysterious. His eyes seemed to dart back and forth as if making sure no one was following him, then quickly rushed into a nearby alley.

"Marshall!" I gasped in a hushed tone. "I think I just saw the man we met this morning!"

"Yeah, and?" He was still involved in conversation with Jacob and Catherine.

"I'm serious! Shouldn't he still be back at the house? It's only been an hour since we saw him at the cabin!"

"Are you sure it was him?" he asked, as if only to humor me.

"Yes! And he was acting very shifty! He just disappeared into that alley!

Marshall glanced toward the alley then looked at the other two. "Okay, we'll take a look, but I don't think we are gonna find anything. This isn't the movies, you know." So, we all walked toward the alley to investigate.

When we got to the alley, there was no one in sight. The man had vanished. All we saw was a few overflowing trash cans. We were about to turn back when we heard a faint groan. Then, suddenly, what we thought was a big black bag of trash began to move.

Marshall and Jacob instinctively motioned for Catherine and me to stay behind them and walked forward into the alley. "Stay behind us. We don't know who did this or what this guy did to warrant a beating, but whoever did this can't be far away and we don't know what they'd do to us if they knew we saw."

"We didn't see anything!" I whispered in protest.

"They don't know that." Marshall warned. "For all they know, we might have videotaped the whole thing. Now, I'm sure this guy would really appreciate it if we quit bickering before he bleeds out."

I yielded. He was right. We cautiously walked in the direction of the man. "Hello!" Marshall called out. "Who's there?" The man in the trash pile groaned again.

◆ ◆ ◆

When we had reached the trash pile, we began to remove the big, bulky bags of trash that had fallen over the man when he was thrown to the ground. When we finally reached him, we gasped at the sight of the gory-looking bruises that covered his body. We couldn't imagine how all this damage could have been done in such a short time. Whoever had done this must have been pretty livid with this poor man. What could he have done to warrant such a beating? I shook my head as if it would help me focus.

"Hello, can you hear me?...Sir, can you hear me?" Marshall hollered as he shook the man by the shoulders gently. He realizes that this was indeed the man we met merely an hour ago, Nathaniel. Then looking up at me, he said, "Who has a cell phone handy?" Catherine pulled hers out immediately and held it up.

"Great. Go over there, so you can see the street signs, and dial 9-1-1," he said, pointing toward the exit of the alley.

When she had left, he looked over at Jake, and asked, "Do you live nearby?"

"No, but my office is right down the street. It should still be open because a group of my co-workers are pulling an all-nighter to try to finish up some drafts for a new client."

"Okay, we need some stuff to clean him up with. Whatever you got. Bandages, if you have any. If not, any clean fabric and some water. Take Sam with you. I'll stay here, and see if I can wake him up. And hurry!"

"But, what about the attackers? You said they might still be around," I asked, concerned.

He looked up at me, an affectionate look on his face, but said in a soothing voice, "Don't worry about me. I will be just fine. Jacob may need someone to help carry everything."

My brother had never been the macho type. He was never afraid to let you know how much he cared. That was one of the things I had always admired about him. In fact, I had a sneaking suspicion that this was his way of getting me out of the line of fire.

I gave Marshall a look to let him know I was not happy that he was sending me with Jake, much less alone. He looked back at me, as if to say, *'You got a better idea?'* I thought about the possibility of the men who had done this being nearby, and shuddered. *It's for the best. Marshall can handle those guys a lot better than I could,* I told myself. Reluctantly, I followed Jake, as he led me out the alley and toward his office. *At least we won't be alone for long,* I thought.

Chapter Five

It took us about seven minutes, walking at a quick pace to get to Jake's office. We were greeted at the door by a woman who, I assume, was the receptionist, because she was casually perched atop, (That's right, *atop,* not behind) a desk about two feet away from the door, filing her finger-nails. She was sipping what I assumed to be her thirtieth cup of coffee of the day. She pushed a thick blonde curl out of her eye, only for it to fall right back into her eye half a second later.

I must have been staring at her, because Jake startled me by snap-ping his fingers about an eighth of an inch from my nose reminding me of the urgent situation that brought us here in the first place. He signaled for me to follow him as he led me to a corner office.

As soon as we were at the doorway of the enormous office that I knew beyond a shadow of a doubt in my mind that this was Jake's office. It was sort of like what you would describe as an "organized mess." Over the years, Jake had patented the organizational skills that no one else could figure out, though many have tried. It was clear of litter for the most part, except for the stacks as tall as myself of newspapers that dated back as far as the 1950's. He'd always been interested in journalism, but not any fluff stories or advertisements. Ever since he was a young child, he'd al-ways dreamed of reporting on the biggest front-page story in history. So, he read every paper he could get his hands on for the past ten years, and never had the heart to throw a single one away.

"Still haven't kicked that old habit, huh?" I said as I slid my fingers across a paper from the summer of 1985 that he had laminated.

"Never," he said as he opened and closed a couple of his desk draw-ers. *Still the same old Jake,* I thought, nodding. Jacob had been collect-ing newspapers since he was about thirteen. I never understood it.

"I found some gauze," he said, pulling me back to the present. "I guess Deanna, my secretary, probably got sick of having to go to the store every time I came back to the hub with one injury or another. There should be some tape in the top right-hand drawer. There you go." I pulled out a full dispenser.

"And grab the bottle of bourbon out of that bottom drawer, would you?" he said, a little too casually as he picked up a few clean microfiber rags from a nearby stack. I paused right in the middle of what I was doing, and looked over to see if he was kidding.

"This is hardly the time for liquor, don't you think?" Clearly amused at my youthful naiveté, he crossed the room toward me, put his big hands on my arms, leaned over and gave me a light peck on the cheek. I should have been but definitely was not expecting a gesture like this from him, so all I could do was just stand there. Then, he locked eyes with me. "To clean the wounds," he said with the smirk of a little boy who had just gotten away with something.

I narrowed my eyes at him, twisted from his grasp, and bent down to the drawer to get the bourbon and hide my now flushed cheeks. Even though I knew him well enough to know that this was just his way of being friendly, it still made me feel very uneasy that, even though I had successfully closed this door a few years ago, like the snap of my fingers or a peck on the cheek, he was back in my life, and still driving me crazy just the same as he always did.

Once I had regained my composure, I stood back up, and we proceeded to head back out of the office. We made our way across the building, passed up the group of crammers, squeezed past the highly-caffeinated receptionist, swing open the door, and made the mad dash back to Marshall and the injured Nathaniel.

◆ ◆ ◆

When we rounded the corner into the alley, we were surprised to find Catherine and a strange man kneeling down next to Nathaniel.

"Shouldn't the paramedics be here by now? And, Where's Marshall?" I asked. Catherine was taking Nathaniel's pulse and recording it on a small tablet she had taken from her purse. She held out her hand for help up. I gave her a tug up and waited impatiently for an answer to my questions.

"The paramedics are all tied-up right now," she said, brushing the dust from her clothes. "There was a massive accident downtown. I heard mention of about seven cars and a semi-truck." We all grimaced at the thought. She continued, "They said the best course to take would be for us to drive him to the emergency room ourselves. Then, before I was off the phone, your brother jumped up and volunteered to get his car, but was concerned for my safety here alone. I told him I would call my brother Jeremy to come and sit with me while I wait.

At first sight, there was no mistaking that these two were related. Like his sister, he appeared to take very good care of himself. His light brown hair was coiffed in such a way that you almost couldn't help wanting to run your fingers through it, combing it away from his trance-inducing sea-green eyes. As if this wasn't enough, he had a jaw that looked as if it had been sculpted by Michelangelo Buonarroti himself. And all this was perfectly perched atop a strapping six-foot stature.

"Hello," I said, shaking his outstretched hand. I hadn't noticed before, but he had the arms of Hercules, muscles everywhere. It seemed that this man had hit the genetic lottery, so much so that it was almost too much to bear! "I'm Samantha Palmer." When I said this, it came out admittedly a little bit more weakly than I had hoped. I recovered myself the best I could, then turned to Jake. But, before I could say anything more, he piped up.

"Jacob McAnelly." he said, seeming quite uncomfortable, though I couldn't account for a reason. Suddenly, I remembered that we were all here for a specific purpose, so I turned my attention to the wounded Nathaniel.

"Did Marshall give any specific instructions as to how to treat these wounds?" I asked, pushing a strand of hair back away from my face and kneeling next to Nathaniel to get my bearings. I looked up at Catherine and Jeremy, who, in turn, looked at one another, then, back at me as if to say, "Nothing we can think of." Beginning to panic, I thought to myself, *What have I gotten us into?* I then checked my phone to see if he had called or sent me a text message with his instructions. Nothing.

Much to my relief, as if reading my mind, Jake bent down next to me with the supplies we had brought from his office. "We had better be glad he's unconscious, because this stuff is 100 proof and guaranteed to burn like crazy," he said, as he unscrewed the cap, poured a shot onto one of the rags, then handed it to me.

"Sammy, you start on those wounds on his face." he ordered. I obeyed, feeling a sudden sense of urgency as if I was hit by a shot of adrenaline that only an emergency can bring on (you know, unless you're some kind of secret agent or something).

By the time we had examined, sanitized and bandaged the majority of Nathaniel's trampled body, we were relieved to see that Marshall had returned with the station wagon. Once he had pulled over as close to the alley as he could manage, he hopped out and ran around to open the passenger door. Jake and Jeremy picked up the injured man as best they could, trying not to inflict even more damage to his already badly wounded body, and carefully got him into the truck.

Chapter Six

The next morning, I awoke to the sound of a lively tennis match in the neighboring yard on the other side of us that seemed to be about two feet from my window. With a groggy yawn, I decided to give up the idea of getting back to sleep. I pushed back the covers, revealing my very worn clothes from the day before. Slowly, the remembrance of the previous night flooded from the back of my mind, producing a great discomfort from the depths of my heart. I crawled out of bed. The floor was very cold to my feet, so I skittered over to where my fluffy, warm slippers were, then padded out to the kitchen to get myself some coffee.

Marshall was already up, sitting at the kitchen table on the house phone. When he saw me walk by with my coffee, he told whoever was on the other end of the line to hold on for a minute, then addressed me. "Good morning, sleepyhead. I was beginning to wonder if I should go check your pulse. You were out cold by the time I went in to say good-night last night. You were about to sleep the whole day away."

As I poured coffee in my cup, I yawned and said, "It can't be that late." My husky morning voice was barely recognizable. Coffee in hand, I sat down in the chair adjacent to him. When he held out his watch that indicated that I had slept until a quarter to noon, I laid my head on the table in disgust. He patted my head in sympathy, then turned his attention back to the phone.

"Sorry about that. Sam just got up...Yeah, that's what she thought too..." I picked my head up and silently gestured to ask who he was talking to. He covered the phone receiver and whispered the word "Sarge."

Not quite awake enough to have an intelligent conversation, I stood up to go out to the patio with my coffee. I just whispered, "Tell Dad hi for me." He did so, then had to pull the phone away from his ear, as a clearly audible "HELLO, KITTEN!" came from the other end. *What is it with parents and phones?* I half-smiled, then continued on my previous course. Marshall grabbed my arm gently.

He released my arm once he had my attention and covered the receiver. "Beth and Joe had some business to attend to in the city. They left early this morning and said not to wait up, so it's just us today, okay?" I nodded.

The back porch wasn't much to look at in itself, but it overlooked a courtyard-like area that Aunt Beth and Uncle Joe kept very well-manicured. There were lots of beautiful pansies, peonies and hydrangeas with a birdbath right in the middle. I watched as two little birds bathed themselves in the shallow water, maneuvering around each other like a ballet of nature. It really was a nice thing to look at as a change from the norm of the front porch. I opted to sneak back there to drink my coffee and let the men chat.

After about twenty minutes in this calm, serene setting, I got up and proceeded to go back inside, thinking, hoping that Marshall and my dad had finished their little pow-wow. Of course, they hadn't. Marshall was still sitting in the same place, in the same position as before. Knowing that I couldn't avoid having the phone handed to me eventually, I passed up the table and went to refill my cup.

When I had replenished my coffee, once again, I pulled up the bench across from Marshall. As if on cue, the next words that came from his mouth were "Yes, she just came back in." Not even two seconds later, Marshall pushed the phone in my direction. I swallowed another gulp of coffee, took a deep breath and picked up the phone.

"Hi, Daddy."

"Hello, there, sleepyhead. I heard you had a pretty eventful night." *Like there was nothing else in the whole world to talk about.*

"Yeah, it was definitely eventful, to say the least." I grasped my cup of coffee like a rescued shipwreck victim grasps a life raft.

◆　◆　◆

The ride to the hospital had been very awkward, to say the least, on top of the intense situation at hand. The two men had laid Nathaniel out in the cargo section in the back of the old station wagon. Naturally, Marshall drove, but the trick was where to put the rest of us. And, since Catherine and Jeremy were the native New Yorkers who knew where they were going, they would obviously be the right choice for the office of co-pilots. So, Jacob and I were left to the backseat to keep an eye on Nathaniel's welfare.

When we had finally made it to the emergency room, which was, by the way, not a moment too soon, the place was a madhouse. There were nurses and doctors running about every which direction, gurneys everywhere, being pushed at a runner's pace through double-doored hallways, some surrounded by several anxious loved ones. Frantic patients bobbed and weaved their way through the throngs of candy-stripers huddled together in a defensive sort of manner, though seeming rather indifferent to their surroundings.

"Wow, it's like bedlam in here. That accident must have been pretty messy," remarked Catherine, eyes widened at the marvelous scene.

"I think you might be right," Jeremy added from behind her.

Throughout our time in the waiting room, Nathaniel slipped in and out of consciousness every few minutes, and would mumble a few incomprehensible syllables before falling back into his blacked-out state.

Within a few minutes, a kindly young nurse sauntered over, holding a large clipboard. "We're going to need some information from him. Are you all family?" She directed her question to Marshall, who was using all his energy to keep Nathaniel from falling on the floor.

I stepped forward and spoke in Marshall's behalf. "No. Actually, we just happened to be in the right place at the right time." I know it was a cliched answer but I felt unsure of what else to say. This time, Jacob stepped in. Nothing could have prepared me for what happened next.

"Actually, I am his son," he said with a rather serious look on his face. I couldn't believe what I was hearing. I had never heard Jacob tell such a bald-faced lie as this.

When he and I were together all those years ago, I had learned a lot about his family; that his mother had passed away during childbirth and that his father was not in the picture at the time. He had been in the system from infancy. I'd always assumed that his father had passed away a long time ago. That was really the only scenario I could accept. I couldn't imagine that a father could just leave a child like that. It never entered my mind that he might have a father out there somewhere. Then again, it was really no longer any of my business.

Perhaps he was telling the truth. If so, the next few days were going to be a roller coaster ride for him. What would he do if Nathaniel didn't make it? If all the effort he'd put forth to find and get to know this man came to nothing?

I couldn't hide my shocked expression as I watched the nurse hand the paperwork over to him just like that without any further questioning after my statement. One of us had to be lying, but then again, paperwork must be done.

"But, I have a bit of a dilemma. You see, all of my father's information was left back at his house in his desk."

"Well, I guess we'll do our best to treat him and just cross our fingers that there is nothing else is wrong with him." She bent over to listen to his heart and lungs and shined a small light in both of his eyes.

"Thank you, miss. I will try to get all the information you need from his house in the morning."

"Okay, I will give you some time to fill out what you can of the forms while I see about getting your father a room. My name is Arianna, by the way, and I will be your father's nurse until midnight."

"Jacob." He held out his free hand for the nurse to shake while staring confusedly at the chart that was now in his hand. He sat down in one of the chairs while the rest of us stood around expectantly, watching all the personnel scurry about in their various activities. Once the nurse had brought a gurney and two rather large orderlies to get Nathaniel into it, Marshall led me firmly but tenderly by the arm toward the outer doors of the hospital. When we were a short distance away from the entryway of the hospital, he turned to me with that stern "big brother" look on his face. "I saw that look on your face and I'm pretty confident that I know what you're feeling right now and I sympathize with you. Really I do, but it doesn't matter right now. There are some things you don't know and probably even some things *he* doesn't, but all of that stuff doesn't matter right now because our best friend is in there dealing with something terrible and he needs us more than we need answers, okay?"

My head was really reeling now. "What? What do you know that I don't?"

"He's my friend too, not just your ex. I don't have time to explain now. We need to get back in there and support Nathaniel *and* Jacob, alright?"

With a deep, reluctant sigh, I acquiesced as he began to lead me back inside the waiting room. Once inside, we found only Catherine standing near one of the hallway entrances. "They moved Mr. Grey to a room upstairs. Jacob went with him, Jeremy is over there making a phone call to his office, and I'm here waiting for him and you two." Right as she finished speaking, Jeremy rejoined his sister and proceeded to lead us in the direction of the elevators. Miraculously, we had it all to ourselves. It's always awkward for me to share an elevator with strangers. Both elevators had opened up at the same time, but the left one had four people plus a woman on a stretcher so, naturally, we opted for the empty one.

Once in the elevator, I headed straight for a corner, being that I had no idea where we were going. Jeremy pushed the second floor button.

"They have him in room 231. Let's see... I believe it's in that direction." He pointed to the left as we exited the elevator on the second floor. I held onto Marshall's arm for emotional support as we came near to Jacob, who was standing in the hallway outside Nathaniel's room.

"They're helping him change into a hospital gown right now. Sam, I know I should have said something-"

I held up my hand to let him know that if wasn't necessary to apologize. "All that matters is that Nathaniel gets the help he needs right now."

Marshall squeezed my hand with approval, then leaned over to do one of those weird hugs men do with one another that lasted like half a second. "How are you holding up, buddy?"

He shrugged. "It's like Sam said. At least he's being taken care of now and that's all that matters."

"Your father will see you now," said one of the nurses as she, the orderlies and a security guard exited the hospital room carrying a see-through bag that held Nathaniel's clothes. "You kids did a pretty good job of patching up those wounds. I'll come back shortly with some salve and fresh dressings for him."

"Thank you miss," Jacob said. Then with a sidelong glance in our direction, he said, "Here goes nothing."

I winced at the sight of the fretful look on his face as he took a deep breath to bolster his courage to take the three steps into the hospital room. "Wait," I said and then stepped forward, wrapped my arms around his neck and hugged him tight. I wanted to say something to encourage him. "We're here if you need us" was all I could come up with. He held me for a few more seconds before releasing.

"Thanks." With renewed courage, he walked right into the hospital room.

Marshall then turned and aimed our small group in the direction of the second-floor waiting room. "We should give Jacob some time alone with his father."

Chapter Seven

Over the next few hours, we each took turns sitting with Nathaniel and Jacob while the others of us sat patiently in the waiting room, pouring over every magazine that we could find, trying to keep our minds off of what could be happening at this very moment, with Nathaniel's vitals going up and down like numbers on the stock market, with the men that put him in this condition still out there somewhere, and wondering if they had seen us help poor Nathaniel and whether or not they would now be coming after us. There were so many questions that needed answering and Nathaniel was the key to the answer, but we also needed to focus on Jacob and what he was feeling at this very moment.

What are you doing? You are going to drive yourself crazy if you stay in your head like this. I've got to think of something constructive to do to get my mind busy. As I was pondering what I could do to pass the time, my stomach gave a deafening growl. *That's it! I can get myself something to eat!* But brilliance quickly turned into disappointment as I realized that it was now 6:30 and the cafeteria was closing soon.

As if hearing my thoughts, Jacob emerged from the hallway to the room, looking ragged yet dutifully preoccupied. "Well, we should probably head back home. I've got a lot of stuff to sort out at the house, then I'll be back here in the morning."

So, after picking up some food at an all-night drive-through and dropping off Catherine and Jeremy at his truck back at the alley, Marshall, Jacob and I pointed the old station wagon in the direction of the cabins.

Once we got back to the cabins, it was already dark. Knowing that Nathaniel lay in that hospital bed, helpless as a newborn and at the mercy of the medical staff, who were doubtless walking on eggshells considering the situation, made our resolve to help Jacob through this ever stronger. Determinedly, we proceeded straight to the office to go through everything and look for whatever we could find to help the doctors determine the best way to treat Nathaniel, as well as give us some clue as to whatever he was into that caused someone to want to do something like this to him.

"It just doesn't make any sense!" Jacob exclaimed at one point. "I know that I don't know my father very well, but the one thing I'm sure of is that the man I've been getting to know these past few months wouldn't hurt a fly."

"Well, I only met him yesterday, but I have the sneaking suspicion that you're right," Marshall answered from his tidy little spot amidst the sea of papers all over the floor. "But, there's something we're missing in this whole thing and we need Nathaniel alive to find out what it is." His face was shadowed with determination.

"Thank you, Captain Obvious," grunted Jacob snidely.

"Hey, I was trying to give a compliment," Marshall replied defensively.

"Alright," I admonished. "We are not going to get anywhere if we begin to argue like children." Apparently seeing the wisdom of my argument, the veins in their necks began to relax. "Now, why don't we take a break and get another pot of coffee going?"

Glancing at his watch, then at the medical papers that had been gathered together, Jacob made a counter offer. "Actually, I think we have the information we need for the hospital at least. We should get some rest. It's been a long day."

◆ ◆ ◆

"Samantha?" The sound of my father's worried voice on the other end of the line snapped me back into the present. I shook my head and took a deep breath.

"Sorry, dad. I just got a little distracted." While in my trance, I hadn't noticed that Marshall had gotten up from the table. Now, he emerged from the bedroom, fully dressed, and signaled for me to get off the phone. "Hey, dad, I have to go. Love you guys. Bye."

"Okay, love you too, sweetie. B-" I hung up the phone before he could finish and turned my questioning expression to him.

"We've got to get down the hospital. Jake called. Nathaniel is stable and ready to talk. We are all going to ride up there together. Now, hurry up and get dressed. I'll warm up the wagon."

I got up and hurried straight to the closet. *Eek, it's about time to do laundry.* My side of the closet was mostly bare except for a light pink top that was a little dressy for the occasion, but I thought, *What the heck?* I paired it with some blue jeans to make it slightly more casual, ran my fingers through my hair and called it good. I grabbed my purse and began to head out, then decided to get my book so I grabbed it, shoved it into my purse and ran out the door as fast as I could.

The two men were already standing outside the car. When they caught a glance of my ensemble, the looks on their faces said it all. "Not a word." I pointed a warning finger at them. They threw their arms up in surrender. When I passed them up heading to the right rear seat, I heard a faint whistle. I glared at Jacob. "Just get in the car already."

"Sor-*ry*. It's just that I haven't seen you wear that shirt since high school," Jacob defended himself. "You still wear it quite well." Marshall snickered.

On the ride to the hospital, I caught Jacob peering back through his visor mirror at me several times. I tried my best to ignore him as I pulled out my book to read on the hour-long drive.

♦ ♦ ♦

Our arrival at the hospital, once again, was not a moment too soon. We hurried up to Nathaniel's room in anxious anticipation of what he had to say. We must have all looked like vultures circling their prey when Nathaniel opened his eyes to see us all standing over his hospital bed.

We all said our hellos, and found a place to sit. Finally, Jake asked the question that was on everyone's mind.

"The nurse said you had something to talk to us about? Why did those men beat you up?"

He opened his mouth, but at first no words came out. I could tell that he was carefully weighing what he should say. Finally, he cleared his throat and began. "All will be revealed in time." He waved a hand dismissively. Suddenly, a wide smile brightened his face. "I can't think of those days without getting emotional," he said between heavy breaths. "We don't even hint at the past, let alone discuss it in detail. Journalists, family and strangers of all sorts have all tried to reopen the old wounds so as to examine them and satisfy their hunger for drama; a good story, you know."

All of us were stunned at his words. What was so dire, had been so catastrophic that it, even now, held so much power?

"I'm an old man now and I am tired of running from it. I always knew that there was no avoiding the inevitable. It seems I have to tell someone, specifically all of you. For, you are all more involved than you think you are. But, for now, you must listen to my instructions: You all must be alert, stay together as much as you can, and avoid strangers at all cost. All will be revealed to you in time, but now I must rest. I was given a mild sedative earlier, so I've been taking short naps here and there."

We all shuffled out to the waiting room to give him some space. *Now what? We have no idea how long he might sleep, or even if he would make it through to tell the rest of the story. And what did he mean by saying that we are all involved? And why won't Marshall tell me what he knows? We tell each other everything. What could he possibly have to hide?* Suddenly, a thought popped into my head. I didn't know why, but I wondered if this could have anything to do with what Uncle Joe has been secretively working on in the shed. It certainly would explain a whole lot. And, if it were true, it would mean that I knew something that no one else knew about. This information made me feel a little better so, with a satisfied smile, I got comfortable in the waiting room chair and picked up a magazine.

It wasn't long, however, until we were summoned by a nurse and ushered back into Nathaniel's room. We all got relatively comfortable once again and waited for Nathaniel to finish his story.

"I was living in that house the first time I saw your mother, all thanks, as I'm sure you have figured out, to your aunt and uncle," he said, pointing to Marshall and me. "They were so generous as to let me stay in the house as long as I wanted for a very low rent. They became my very close friends." He shifted his gaze from Marshall to me to Jacob. "Anyway, your mother was from the other side of the lake. We met one perfect summer day in an empty lot in the neighborhood where youths of all ages went to play. She hit me in the gut with a Frisbee," he said as a smile curved one side of his mouth upward. "That was nothing compared to what that girl did to me on the inside. From day one, I was hers and all the signs seemed to say that she was mine too. But, her family had other ideas. You see, there had recently been some small-scale thefts in the area and no one knew who was to blame. Your mother's family had everyone fooled. Their appearance was as a normal, albeit *very* close-knit family. No one suspected their family of such brazen crime as they had committed. Needless to say, they did not want anybody sniffing around and finding out what they had been up to. The day she brought me home, they were furious. They forbade her from ever seeing me again. I was so distraught that I fled to Joe and Beth's house at once. They were so kind and affected and, might I say, quite the romantics. They swore to me their secrecy, should there ever be another confrontation. They warned me that if I even thought of coming around again, there would be consequences."

It was at this time that his speech was interrupted by the entrance of a nurse in clean, fresh blue-green scrubs, wielding a fresh IV bag filled with a clear fluid. "Hello, Mr. Grey. My, you sure have a lot of company! Are you all family?" She seemed rather taken aback by our presence. It was as if, as soon as she saw us, she got very tense. Call it a bit alarmist or what have you, but I wasn't sure what to think of this. It all seemed a bit shifty to me. I kept my gaze on her as she walked past me toward toward the bed.

"Well, my dear, this handsome young man in the chair nearest me is my son, Jacob. And these two are friends of the family," he said with a smile in my direction. "Now, what have you got for me, nurse?"

"Oh, I'm just here to change out your intravenous therapy bag. This will only take a moment. Then, you can get back to your visitors. The doctor authorized a change in your treatment. It should take effect in a short while."

Nathaniel looked confused. "I don't recall him mentioning any change in medication."

"Well," she stammered, "The order just came through a few moments ago." Apparently blind to the eeriness that I was seeing, he waved a hand dismissively.

"These doctors nowadays never tell you what they're up to. You could be injecting me with cyannide for all I know." This comment only resulted in a slight snicker.

We watched as she quickly took the bag that was still half-full off the IV pole and placed the new bag, then switched out the tube from the port in his arm. This led me to conclude that nursing is not for the squeamish. I cringed as I watched this seemingly simple procedure, the few drops of blood that inevitably came into the tube from the needle as it was attached. The utter force she did this procedure with, though, made us all groan. Then, just as suddenly as she entered, she turned and made her way out of the little hospital room. As she exited the room, I seemed to note a slight darkness to her expression that made me think that Nathaniel's accusation could hold some weight. I could not stay silent. As soon as the 'nurse' was out of earshot, I jumped up. "Nathaniel, you're not the least bit leery of whatever that nurse just gave you? I would think an actual professional might give you a *little* bit more information than that before she stuck a tube in your hand! I did *not* like the looks of her at all."

Chapter Eight

Within half an hour, we had no doubt of our suspicions being correct. Nathaniel began to sweat profusely, his breathing became rapid and labored, his body convulsed and the machines started making so much noise I was sure it could be heard back in Texas. A few panic-stricken seconds went past before what seemed like a crowd of various kinds of medical professionals rushed into the room with a large table of equipment, practically pushing us out into the hallway. Almost before we were out of the room, the door was slammed shut with a resounding thud. We were all a bit shell-shocked as we stood out in the hall looking from one to the other of our companions. Not knowing what else to do, we all clasped hands with me in the middle and made our way to the waiting room. All the emotional baggage, all awkwardness that this might have previously caused seemed to melt away, as the weight of situations such as this tended to make happen. We held on tight to the hands of one another until we reached the waiting room. We sat in the only place where three chairs together were empty. I leaned on Marshall's shoulder and stayed that way until a highly scrubbed-up doctor emerged from the hallway. Everyone in the room who had been waiting for news of their own loved one's well-being, seemed to draw in their breath simultaneously.

"Nathaniel Grey's family," he said, gravely. We all stood, clinching every muscle in our collective bodies and clasped hands once again.

"I am his son, and this is my support team," Jacob said, although he didn't really have to clarify. If this wasn't the definition of a family, I don't know what is.

The doctor's eyes fell for a second, then he continued, waving us in the direction of a nearby room. We all filed into the room that turned out to be an unoccupied patient room. If you ask me, he looked even more uneasy than Jacob. He shuffled his feet a little and finally spoke. "Look, there's no easy way to tell you this, but I believe your father was poisoned." We all gasped. "If appears that whoever beat him must've also tried to poison him once they found out he was here."

"There's no way the nurse we saw was the one who beat him. She was older and sort of frail."

"Then, it could be that we have an accomplice among our staff. In that case, what I suggest we do is get him out of here very quickly and without a discharge form, so as not to alert the culprit that we're onto her. Wait here." He disappeared from the room for about a minute and a half. When he came back, he had two small bottles and a straw in his hands. "This is activated charcoal. It tastes horrible but it will draw the poison from his body. It will take about a day for him to pass it and his stool will look a little funky but he should be fine."

My head was reeling. So many thoughts were scrambling for a tether hold, I didn't know what to do. As I looked around the room at each of the people that occupied it, I could see all the little wheels turning in their heads, but no one said a word. Silencing my mind, so as to stop it from spinning so I could make an intelligible decision if need be, would be nearly insurmountable, an Olympic Gold medal-worthy feat, but I must focus, because Nathaniel's life depended on it. There was so much to be done and all of it had to be done quickly and without the knowledge of the medical staff or anyone else.

Looking around in the hall, I saw that the hospital was buzzing with activity, so it wouldn't be hard, if we focused, to execute the plan that was forming in my head. I began to look back and forth between the three men. I tugged at Marshall's arm. "What if we were to, say, replace Nathaniel's body with a, um, decoy, so to speak?"

"Oh," said Marshall. "I like the way you think." We looked toward the doctor, who smiled at me appreciatively.

"This girl's got a good head on her shoulders. Sounds like you've got this under control. Get to it and I will handle the staff, so that you shouldn't have too much trouble." With that, he left the room to us.

After I told them my plan, Marshall looked over to me dutifully. "You have your cell phone?" I nodded toward my purse. He shook his head. "That's not close enough. Stick it somewhere on your person and I'll take your purse down to the station wagon. Oh, and no back pockets. That's the surest way to get it lifted." I obediently proceeded to take my cell phone out of its pocket and, to the guys' horror, stuffed it in my bra. Once the men had recovered from their horror, he continued, "Jake, you go with her down to the morgue. It shouldn't be too hard to figure out this transfer. I'll make sure Nathaniel is taken care of in the meantime."

We all hurried off to our respective tasks. Getting into the morgue was way easier than it should have been. Hasn't anyone heard of security? I'm not even from the city and I'm able to get in here. It was pretty unnerving, but we trudged onward.

"Whoever we find can't be in too unnatural a position already, because we will have to be able to position him in some way so as to look like a fresh body," I instructed. "Good thing there's only an IV to take out of Nathaniel's arm. I hope Marshall remembers to turn off the machine before taking the IV out, so the alarms don't start going off." Jacob only nodded.

"So, how do we go about checking these bodies?" he asked. Just as I began to reply, I heard elevator doors open and close. Marshall wouldn't have come down for us, would he? I was sure he couldn't imagine the horror that we were experiencing in this very instant. This was a million times worse than thinking about the fact that we were surrounded by bodies. Even if we crouched behind a table, we would be seen in a matter of seconds. Jacob leaned down and whispered in my ear. "We can tell them we just came to pay our last respects."

"Uh... uh...okay I guess," was all I could muster, as my body began to shake all over. Jacob swiftly and instinctively stepped between the elevator and my, a protective arm outstretched.

And then, there was a cessation of footsteps as this person paused right outside the morgue door. I could feel my heart racing. I held onto my tears as I felt a bead of sweat trickle from my forehead. We heard the doorknob turn, the door open and finally a man's voice say "I know you're in here and you have no reason to be afraid. I'm alone and would like to speak to you before anything else is done. Won't you allow me to come in?" I clinched my fist.

"Alright, come in," Jacob said, bracing himself.

"I'm not going to turn on the light either. You are safe, but the less you see of me for now, the better for all parties. I'm here to help you. I've been asked by someone to replace Nathaniel in that hospital bed. As soon as you leave the room, I will slip in through the window. It has been arranged for a path to be cleared for your departure. Now, go and don't ask questions. Once you are in the clear, point your car West and don't stop until you run out of gas. Goodbye for now. We shall meet again under better circumstances." As a gloved hand appeared from the shadows, we took a collective deep breath and reluctantly shook it. As I shook, a small piece of paper was pressed into my hand.

Chapter Nine

The sequence of events that happened next seemed to happen a lot more smoothly than it should have. I was much more nervous than thankful due to that fluidity. We were all safe and sound in the station wagon before we knew it and Nathaniel was resting quite comfortably laid out in the back seat. In all the movement and commotion, there had been no sound from him except breathing. Good.

We were all a bit on edge still as we headed West. We followed the GPS as far as direction, though our real destination was a mystery to us all. We looked from one to the other of our companions for a clue.

"Go west. That's all we were told," Jacob said. Marshall, who was driving for the first leg of the night just shrugged.

"Okay then, we all got our cell phones?"

"Yes, sir," said Jacob. Next, Marshall looked over to me. I smiled and looked down toward my chest where my phone was still snugly tucked in place.

"I'm good." I said, grinning at the faces they both made.

"Okay, then. Let's save the juice on them. I'm not exactly sure where we will end up, but here we go nonetheless. We can check in with anyone we want to when we get to a stopping place."

Nathaniel was sound asleep. He looked quite comfortable, despite the pain I was sure he must be feeling from his wounds. He was sprawled across the back seat, his head in Jacob's lap, filling up as much of the space as humanly possible. Listening for his breathing wasn't a problem either, for this was slightly elevated in his sleeping state. Still, it was a relief that he was feeling stable enough to sleep for the time being. At the hospital, he had been given an injection to slow the effects of the poison and another dose of the sedative.

As for the rest of us, we spent the next five minutes of the ride with every eye on the road, though if any animals were to cross the road in front of us, not one of us would see it. It was more of a dead-eyed stare as the reality of the preceding occurrences set in.

Just when it seemed like no one could stand the silence any longer, my phone vibrated, as if to provide me with an out in this frantic situation. I got it out of my pocket, where I had moved it earlier when no one was looking and was surprised to find that Jake had sent me a text message.

> *I'm sorry.*

I looked back at him. He was sitting in a pretty uncomfortable position, Nathaniel's head now resting on one leg, looking down at his phone. I began typing my reply.

> *What are you talking about? You were right. I need to make more decisions for myself.*

A short time later, he answered.

> *Whatever the case, it was not my place to say. You have every right to say no to me if that's what you REALLY feel is the right thing for you.*

Feeling completely overwhelmed and exasperated that he chose *right now* to have this particular conversation, I gave a great sigh. It wasn't until that moment that he looked up from his cell phone and looked me dead in the eye, as I was looking back at him through my mirror.

> *It's not your fault. This all came at me so fast and without notice. I didn't know what else to do. Give me a little time to think about this.*

I sent the message and looked toward the window to hide the tears that were now welling up in my eyes.

> *Take the time you need. I'll wait. I've done it before and I can do it again.*

Before I could reply, Marshall broke the silence by suggesting that we review the information that the doctor had given us just before we snuck out the back exit of the hospital.

"He mentioned that we might ought to wait until we cross the state line before we make any stops," Jacob said to begin the conversation.

"Sammy, you still got that contact number they gave us for that bed and breakfast?" Marshall asked, looking over at me as I began to search through my purse for the tiny scrap of paper that had been given me to guard with my life. Two minutes later, I came up victorious.

"Aha!" I had found the small yellow paper in the bottom of my purse between my wallet and a lipstick that was too dark for my skin tone.

"Okay, well, perhaps someone else ought to hold on to that," he said, taking it from my outstretched hand and sticking it in his pants pocket while keeping a firm hand on the wheel as he simultaneously swerved into the passing lane, nearly getting rear-ended by an SUV.

"You just pay attention to the road so we can get to our destination in one piece," I said, as I held onto my purse, which had begun to fall due to the sudden lane shift.

◆ ◆ ◆

Over the next hour, there was, yet again, complete silence. Jacob had fallen asleep and Marshall continued to keep his eyes fixed firmly on the road. It was at this time that I decided to examine the scrap of paper that had been given me by the mystery man. *I bet this is just his phone number or something.* I slowly opened the tattered piece of paper.

Aunt Mattie's farm

Hmm? Perhaps he meant this for someone else? Then I rolled my eyes. *Yeah, some other people whose father and friend had been poisoned by some strange woman who had impersonated a nurse.* I folded up the note and put it back in my pocket. I leaned my head against the door and closed my eyes.

When I opened my eyes once again, I sat straight up, my eyes wide. "Marshall!" I exclaimed, causing him to swerve and land right in front of a billboard that had caught my attention.

"Jeez, what is it?!" Marshall exclaimed as he put the station wagon in park and turned to me.

"That billboard!" I exclaimed at their confused faces. I looked toward Jacob, who had woken up with a jolt. "Do you know where that is?" I asked him, pointing to the sign. The sign that had caught my attention read as follows:

> *Need a break from the hustle and bustle of the city?*
> *Come on down to Aunt Mattie's Pick-Your-Own Farm and*
> *Bed-and-Breakfast!*

"Not at all but I have a feeling *you* do," Jacob replied, groggily rubbing at his sleep-addled face.

"No, it's just that when that mysterious man from the morgue shook my hand, there was a piece of paper in it. I think that the plan he referred to calls for us to stay the night there," I nearly shouted, still exuberant about the fact that I had actually figured something out.

"Well, that's good to know now that we are such a short way there."

"Wait a second," Jacob interjected. "Didn't the doctor say to cross the state line?"

"Uh, I don't know about you, but I would go with the person who seemed to be more involved in the situation," I retorted.

"Actually, the doc said a lot more than your mystery man had to say."

"Okay, children," Marshall chastised.

Jacob threw his hands in the air in retreat. "You're right, I guess.

"So, anyone got a hat we can use to pick at random?" Marshall joked.

"I just have this gut feeling that we should try this B-and-B, though I'm not sure why."

"The question is, then, do we trust your gut feeling?" Jacob asked.

After a few silent moments, Marshall made his judgment. "What could it hurt? A bed-and-breakfast sounds fairly harmless. It's not like it's an abandoned warehouse or something."

"This is true." Jacob said.

"Okay then, it's settled." I concluded the conversation as I took a note of the directions from the billboard on a piece of paper that I had found under Marshall's seat. "Who wants to hold onto these?" I asked as Jake held out his hand. I handed him the piece of paper on which I'd listed all the information that the billboard had on it in regard to directions. With that, I leaned back in my seat and prepared for a relaxing ride for the next fifteen minutes toward the bed-and-breakfast.

Sadly, I had no such privilege, as suddenly, the vehicle began to shake more than what was normal. I looked back to see Nathaniel's body seizing and convulsing as the poison hit his digestive system. As it was only moments since Marshall had pulled off the road, I prompted him to pull over again, (much to his annoyance, as he was listening to the news report on the radio) so that I could find some way to have more access to Nathaniel. As soon as the wheels were no longer turning, I jumped out my door and flung open the hatchback with the men on my heels, as soon as they realized what was happening. As there was no safe way of moving him anywhere, we all did our best to restrain him until the convulsions subsided. I checked his pulse and breathed a sigh of relief at his heartbeat, though it was very quick.

"Okay, we just have to keep him alive for the next fifteen minutes. Perhaps this Mattie person will know of a place he can get treatment. Plus, at some point, we need to stop and find a place to pick up some essentials. You know, toothbrushes, toothpaste, deodorant and anything else we can think of that we just can't live without. Just to get us through whenever this thing is over."

The remainder of the ride was hectic to say the least. We had given him the charcoal like the doctor said and he was able to keep it down surprisingly well, even though it looked disgusting and blackened his mouth. But he was still a wreck. He began to hallucinate and, at least we guessed, whatever he was seeing was causing him to thrash about the backseat. At one point, we had to move him to the hatchback for Jacob's safety. When we finally arrived at our destination, our relief was audible, as every one of us exhaled a deep breath, grateful for the possibility of getting Nathaniel the help that he needed.

We pulled into a driveway that was marked with an AM in iron lettering above a road of loose gravel. To each side as we made our way toward the building was a field an acre or so wide with seasonal flowers. It was the kind of sight that made you want to be ten years old again, bounding through brightly-colored flowers that reached to your knees with a basket in your hand, hair flowing freely behind. The inn was larger than I had imagined, reminding me of the "cottages" you would see in 19th century movies and books. It was a beautiful two-story rock building with vines of ivy growing up the side, but somehow not overpowering the building itself.

As if on cue, the same moment that we had found a place to park, a frazzled red-haired woman emerged from the front door in a long, flowing, fleece robe.

"Can I help you?"

Marshall was the first to speak up. "Yes. First of all, we need to find a doctor fast."

"Well, my husband is a doctor. He works at a hospital not far from here. He may be able to help you there."

"Well, it's a little more urgent than that. We have a man with us who has been poisoned. So, we have very little time."

"Poisoned!?" the woman said, "Well, that's a horse of a different col-or! Let me help you kids to a room. We do happen to have a room with a hospital bed. Sometimes, my husband brings some work papers home and spends the night in there. A few times, he's handled a 'sensitive' case and the hospital assigns someone under our care here."

How peculiar, I thought, *Isn't that kinda the opposite of a house call?*

"Here, let me help you kids get settled. I just hate to see you young ones out here in the dead of the night. Don't get me wrong, I'm a modern woman. No eating dinner at two in the afternoon for me, but I'm no night owl either." We all shared a look of disbelief amongst ourselves. Or, at least we hoped it would remain between the three of us, but she must have caught on to us, because she continued. "You just happened to catch me on a night that I'm waiting up for my husband to get home from a late night at work. Here, let me get you kids a pen and paper, and you can write down your friend's symptoms. Then, hope-fully, my husband hasn't left the hospital yet, and he can diagnose what poisons might have been given to your friend according to his symptoms and bring home the appropriate antidote."

"Well, actually, we've already given him some activated charcoal a doctor gave us at a hospital. Thank you so much for offering. I think he just needs to rest."

Of course, dear." said the woman as she turned to-ward the inn, beckoning us to follow her.

"Uh, sis," prodded Marshall, as he gently squeezed my elbow. "I think someone should stay behind with Nathaniel. This was like it was my fa-ther's voice coming out of my brother's mouth. While we were growing up, my father always expressed the important responsibility that he put upon himself and his sons to be the protective sort toward their sisters and, later on, their wives. He never let us children go to strangers' houses on our own. To tell the truth, it does feel rather good to know that you are protected.

And, Marshall was doing the right thing. We did not know this woman, who she was, or what waited for us in-side that door. For all we knew, she and the man who had given us the direction to come here could both be psychopaths just waiting to get some unsuspecting young adults into their grasp. We knew not to go into any house growing up, especially, if the person is particularly persistent.

"Oh, dear. What kind of hostess would I be if I al-lowed a young lady to stand out here in the pitch-dark, cold air? Let me help you get your friend inside. It couldn't be good for him to stay out here either."

I looked questioningly over at Marshall, who only shrugged back.

"By the way, I don't believe we've been introduced. My name is Matilda, but everyone calls me Mattie. Now, you don't have to look so worried. We're all family here." With that, our fears were slightly allayed, so Marshall and Jacob, who had kept silent this entire time, proceeded to open the hatchback door into where Nathaniel still lay and carefully lift him out.

◆ ◆ ◆

Once we had gotten Nathaniel into the hospital bed, the woman had giv-en us the paper and pen. "Perhaps my husband can give him something to make him more comfortable so he can get some rest tonight." So, we sat around the coffee table and proceeded to write down his symptoms, the name of the hospital we had taken him to, and the name of the doctor who helped us get out safely. "There. That should be all the information he will need. I was thinking he could confer with the doctor who helped us get out safely. He may have figured out what was given Nathaniel." Marshall pointed to the name he'd written down.

"Okay," the woman said, shakily taking the piece of paper and walk-ing toward the old-fashioned wall phone. "Oh, here is your room key." She plucked a key of of the wall and tossed it to Jacob. "I'm afraid you'll all have to share our last empty room. There's some sort of convention going on in town, so we have more boarders than usual. Your friend, of course, gets the medical room here on the first floor." With that, she went back to the phone and left us to find our room on our own.

"Well, the key has a nine engraved in it, so I'm guessing it's a safe bet that we are up there," observed Jacob as he pointed up the stairs toward a door directly in front of them marked with a gold number 9. We continued up the stairs, but just as Jacob was about to stick the key into the lock, the door came open on its own! All of a sudden, there stood a tower of a man, looking down at us menacingly. We all took a deep gulp.

Chapter Ten

"Hello, um, sir," Jacob said sheepishly. "I'm sorry. We're a little con-fused. We have a key for room nine also, so we seem to have been double-booked."

With that, the face of a once scary-looking man became the grin of a lifelong friend. "Oh, of course!" He took his finger and turned over the gold number on the door. "That confuses a lot of folks. Room nine is down the hall a few doors. We thanked him and headed down the hall in the direction in which the jovial man had pointed us.

"Here we are. The *real* number nine." Marshall pointed to the door.

Once we were all inside the door, we threw our bags on the floor and collapsed onto the beds, Marshall and Jake on the one nearest the door and me on the one nearest the window.

"What next?" I asked as I watched the ceiling fan move in quick, un-ending circles.

"Next, you two unpack your things while I check on my father and then we will all be sacked out within half an hour." Jacob explained.

"Sounds great but, first, we need to check in with our aunt and tell her we won't be home for a while," Marshall reminded. *Groan!* I got my phone out of my pocket and proceeded to dial. Not wanting to be the person to tell our aunt what was happening, I handed the phone to Marshall, patted his shoulder with gratitude, and proceeded to go down-stairs to check on Nathaniel.

When I got down to the lobby level, it seemed that Nathaniel had al-ready been moved to the little hospital-like room, because the couch and the lobby were both unoccupied. I walked toward the room, but the door was shut, so I decided to just wait patiently. I surely was in no hurry to go back upstairs. I took a seat on the lobby couch and decided to look for something to read. On the table, I found a book about wildflowers, a magazine that featured an article about how to whip your thighs into shape and a book of old family photos. Curious, I picked up the photo album. Most of the pictures were black-and-white. There was one particular woman that was in quite a few of the pictures. *I assume that is Mattie.* I leaned in and squinted my eyes to see if I could come up with any similarities. Though it didn't look that much the way she looks now, the woman's kind eyes and warm smile reminded me of someone, though I couldn't exactly put my finger on who.

"Find anything interesting?" I was suddenly startled as Mattie and Jake entered the room. I felt a knot in my stomach and sort of a deer-in-the-headlights expression spread across my face.

"I'm sorry," I stammered. "I didn't mean to snoop. I just saw this photo book..."I trailed off as Mattie began to chuckle.

"Don't worry about it, dear!" She smiled approvingly. "I put those pictures out there to be looked at."

I breathed a sigh of relief, looking from Mattie to Jacob and back again. "Then, would you mind if I asked you a question?"

"Not at all. What's your question?"

Careful with my phrasing, I continued. "Who is the woman in all these pictures?"

She sat next to me. "That is my sister. She passed away years ago. I keep these pictures out here to preserve her memory. Occasionally, a guest will get bored and pick up that book and I get to tell them all about her."

"Would you mind, then, if I took it into my room for the night? I just love to look at pictures." At this request, she sat up straighter.

"Not at all, dear! Go right ahead." Her words sounded approving, though her expression said something completely different, though I wasn't sure what. I also wasn't sure what I was going to find, but there appeared to be something familiar about this woman, and I was going to get to the bottom of it. I got up with the book and headed toward the stairs.

Then, suddenly, it occurred to me what I had come down here for. I quickly turned around, nearly tripping over my own feet in the process, had Jacob not been right behind me. He leapt to action and swooped to catch me in his arms in a swift motion. He looked at me as if to say *I told you I'd always catch you.*

"Oh, thank you," I couldn't help but say. I straightened myself up. "How's your father doing? Do they know what poison was given him?"

"He's going to be fine. The charcoal is already doing its job and he's gonna be sleeping it off for a little while and be back to normal before we know it."

"Well, that's a relief."

◆ ◆ ◆

When I got back to the room, Marshall was off the phone, stretched across the bed, my phone right next to him. I picked it up. It was open to a message.

> *Take the time you need. I'll wait. I've done it before and I can do it again.*

I looked over at Marshall, shocked.

"Don't give me that look," he said without even turning over, as if he had eyes in the back of his head. "I'm your brother and the closest thing you have to a best friend. You don't think I know what happens right under my nose?"

I stayed quiet for a moment, gathering my thoughts. I laid the phone on my bed and sat. I wanted so badly to talk to him about everything that was going through my head, but I feared that Jacob would just scoff at me like I'd disappointed him.

"Well, I'm going to tell you what I think anyway, even if you don't want to hear it." *Hmm, a loophole. He only meant that I shouldn't ask Marshall's advice, but this is unsolicited advice.* I felt so triumphant. "First off, I'm a little surprised you didn't come to me about this in the first place-"

I cut him off. "When have I had time?"

"Well, you have a point there."

"Besides," I said, "He had some kind of issue about me coming to you."

"Why do you think that is?"

"I don't know, Marshall. When I figure men out, I'll let you know."

"It seems to me that you two have been going back and forth like a bad sitcom, so there's really no stopping you from eventually giving in to your obvious feelings for one another. You just have to make sure you're ready this time. He probably still has a soft spot from the last time you practically left him at the altar."

"I did not leave him at the altar," I retorted with a huff.

"Whatever you want to call it. Anyway, I think we ought to get some rest. Goodnight." He got off the bed, pulled down the covers and crawled in.

"Oh!" I hollered. This time, it was my turn to make him jump out of his skin. I went over to the little table on which I had set the old photo album.

Marshall was right on my heels. "What is it now?" he protested.

"Calm down," I said first. "Earlier, when I was flipping through this photo album, I saw a bunch of pictures of this woman. She looks so familiar. I just can't put my finger on who she looks like."

"Well, did you ever stop to think that maybe she just has one of those familiar faces?"

"No, there's more. Mattie acted very strange when I asked if I could look at this album. I think she may be hiding something. But, why would she have something she wanted hidden laid out where anyone could look at it?"

"Ever heard of hiding in plain sight?"

"I suppose. But *why?*"

"I don't know. I suggest we sleep on it and worry about it in the morning."

"Right behind you."

Just as we were about to go to sleep, Jacob walked in the room.

"What are you so calm about?" I asked lifting my head from my pillow.

"I don't know. I just feel at home for some reason. Maybe it's because I'm with you two and that makes me feel safe."

"There's nowhere we'd rather be," I assured him. Then, I came to a realization. "Wait a minute! Don't move! Marshall, look at this! Do you see what I see?"

"Oh, would you go to sleep already?" Marshall asked crankily. Reluctantly, he turned over. "What is it I'm supposed to be seeing?"

"That woman! The woman in the book!"

"What are you talking about?" Jacob and Marshall asked simultaneously as I hurried over to the table and picked up the book. I grabbed Jacob's chin and put the open book up next to his face.

"Do you see what I'm talking about now?

"Noooo. You're gonna have to spell it out for me, sis."

"There is a definite resemblance between Jacob and the woman in these pictures! That's what I have been seeing this whole time!"

"If you say so. Like I told you before, she could just have one of those faces that're easily mistaken for someone else.

"Yes, but transgender look-alikes? That doesn't happen unless you're family. Jacob, I think we may have just found your mother!"

Chapter Eleven

Marshall and Jacob both looked at me as if trying to figure out if there was merit to my theory or if I was a crazy person.

"Okay, where did you come up with that idea? That was a huge jump?" Jacob raised an eyebrow at me.

"Think about it. You've never seen your mother or any pictures of her. This woman looks exactly like you and you want to let the chance go by?"

"Okay, so what if she is my mother? She passed away years ago, remember? There's no way I could get to know her once I find out the truth."

"Well, we need to..."

"What we need to do first of all is get some rest. All of this will still be here in the morning. Perhaps Matttie will let us poke around a bit-"

"No!" I cut him off. "Mattie must *not* know about this! There's something about her I don't trust."

"Okay then."

◆ ◆ ◆

When I awoke the next morning, the place was quiet, as if there was no one about, though it was already late in the morning. *Perhaps they all went out for their daily activities.* While the men were still lying around lazily, I decided to seize the opportunity to poke around a bit.

At the end of the hallway, there was a staircase that, until now, I had suspected was more rooms. Eyes and ears peeled, I made my way up the somewhat rickety stairs.

I soon found myself in a seemingly very typical dusty old attic. There were boxes marked 'photos' all over the small room, each marked with a different name. One was marked 'Mattie'. Then there was 'Clive', 'Roberta' and a few others. I stepped toward the box marked 'Roberta', opened it and could not believe what I saw. It was the same woman that was in all the other pictures and standing next to her was a man I immediately recognized as Nathaniel! *This is perfect! Exactly what I need to prove to the boys that I'm not crazy!* Without a moment's thought, I seized the picture and shoved it into my pocket.

"Can I help you, miss?" came a calm voice from behind me. I turned on my heels so sharply that I nearly fell over. He swiftly caught me by the arm to steady me.

"I'd be careful, there, miss. I wouldn't want to have to order another hospital bed for you to stay in."

I silently hoped that he hadn't seen my act of novice detective work. Once I regained the ability to both speak and use my legs properly, I said, "Oh, you must be Mattie's husband, the doctor."

"Pleased to make your acquaintance," he said in a friendly manner as he held out a gloved hand. "Don't worry. The glove is clean. I was just about to check on your friend when I heard some noise up here."

I hadn't noticed before but this man had a very distinct look about him. His lab coat and handlebar mustache seemed to contradict one another in style. He wore slacks and a chapeau as well, which made him look like he came straight out of a Dickens novel or something.

"And what, pray tell, might you be doing in my attic?"

I had to think quickly. "Ummm, I was looking for the communal bathroom."

"Oh, dear. Well, right this way, my lady." He gestured back down the stairs with an outstretched arm. The other was offered to me as an idyllic deed of gallantry to help me down the rickety stairs. As we reached the common bathroom, he added, "I don't believe I caught your name, dear."

"Oh yeah. It's Samantha, sir. Samantha Palmer."

"Nice to meet you, miss. I'm Clive. I am Matilda's husband, as you have so cleverly already ascertained. Now, if you'll excuse me, I have some business of my own to attend to."

As soon as he was out of sight, I tiptoed back to the room. Marshall and Jacob were still in the same position I left them in. Thinking they were both asleep, I tiptoed over to the table.

Jacob lifted his head. "Where have you been?"

"In the attic."

"Geez, you went in their attic? How... Why... I don't even know what to say to that!"

"I thought there might be more rooms up there. Jacob, I think there might be something up there that we can use to find out more about your mother."

"*If* she *is* my mother. Remember, we are not sure of anything yet."

"And there is where you're wrong. I believe I have found some pretty solid evidence that supports my theory. This photo pretty much says it all. Take a look." I retrieved the photo from my pocket and handed it to him.

He took it, thoroughly examining it, eyes wide with disbelief. "This doesn't exactly prove anything, you know."

"Well, there's only one way to find out, isn't there? I thought we might poke around up there while everyone is asleep and see what we can find."

"Ugh, fine. As long as we don't have to do anything right now."

"Oh, go back to sleep already. We have another long night ahead of us."

Jake groaned and rolled back over.

While the men sleep the day away, I decided, *I will go downstairs and take a peek at the itinerary for the day. Perhaps I will find something interesting to keep my mind on for the afternoon.*

After searching the itinerary of the bed-and-breakfast for a few moments and finding nothing of interest on there, I decided to wander around for a while. I'd never noticed before now that in the hallway there were rows and rows of photos of a lot of the same people from the photo book. I stood at the top of the stairs where the majority of the pictures were hung for a while. There were pictures of all shapes and sizes yet arranged so nicely. *Mattie must have hung every one of these herself.* I had to hand it to her that she kept a very nice house, with lots to entertain the guests.

When I had examined all the pictures, I proceeded to go back down the stairs to the entrance of the backyard. There was a beautiful stone path that weaved through a large garden. As I walked, I thought a lot about my life and how much things had changed since I'd met Jacob. I thought about the wonderful times we'd had as friends growing up together, how much in love we had once been(and might still be), how he expressed just the right amount of chivalry at the perfect time every time I felt down and needed someone to hold me. He'd always known when I needed a laugh and when I needed a shoulder to cry on. He'd told me once that it was my eyebrows that told him which time was which. But there was a serious side to him that I'd always enjoyed listening to. He seemed to command just enough authority to where people, especially women including myself, seemed to be drawn to following along with him as he read Tennyson or Chaucer or whatever poet he was into at the time. I thought of the way he looked at me as if his heart beating depended on my lips moving along with the words he read to me. For all these things and so many more, I came to a decision that, yes, I was still very much in love with him. But, was I ready to make a commitment to him. That is when I realized that it didn't matter anymore. The love I had for him was now stronger than the force pulling me away, my now faded desire for independence. At that very instant, I turned right around and proceeded determinedly back toward the house. I was going to tell the man that I love that I want to spend the rest of my life with him.

Then, a thought occurred to me. *What if he is still in bed?* I couldn't very well tell him how I felt at such an inopportune time. It had to be perfect.

I continued back to the inn anyway, for I realized that I had wandered quite far.

Just then, I head an eerie voice from behind me speak. *"Stop investigating my family!"*

I stopped dead in my tracks as chills reverberated up and down my spine like a slinky. I felt as if I'd been electrocuted. Not knowing what to do, I looked around to see who was there and saw no one. The weeds on either side of the trail were tall enough that they could shield anyone from view if they did not want to be seen. I kept my eyes peeled so as to see if I could discern anyone from far away. The trees formed a large archway at the fence line of the property. *The perfect escape route. Probably just some kids playing a joke or something*, I tried to convince myself.

When I got back inside, everything was still silent. I wondered if and when anyone was ever coming back. Surely, bird watching didn't take this long. Usually, places like this bustled with activity, but this bed-and-breakfast was certainly unique in character. I looked around for any sign of life on the ground floor. Nothing. Nobody but Nathaniel, who lay sleeping in the little room peacefully. I smiled to myself, then headed toward the stairs to our room.

"Well, what are you children up to this fine day?" came Mattie's voice from behind me. *Spooky*, I thought. I was sure no one was there before.

"Oh, not much. I went for a nice little stroll in the back yard. Just wondering, did y'all have any kids?"

"Oh, no, dear. Sadly, Clive and I never seemed to have the time for children."

"What about Ro- uh, your sister?"

"No, no. She never even married. Poor thing. Say, why so interested in my sister?" My heard skipped a beat or two when I realized I may have given myself away. I took a deep breath and passed it off as a yawn.

"Just making small talk," I said, miraculously able to stay calm. "Well, I may head back up to my room and take a short nap." I *had* to go up and talk to the boys about this.

When I made it back to the room, Marshall was up combing his hair and Jacob was reading a magazine that had been left on the small bedside table between the beds.

"Well, look who's finally decided to join the land of the living," I said, trying desperately to sound nonchalant.

They weren't buying it. Both men put down what they were holding and looked at me. "What happened?" they both asked simultaneously.

"I just had a *very* eerie experience!"

"Well, what was it?" Marshall asked worriedly.

"I don't know. First, there was this voice that came out of nowhere saying to stop investigating Mattie's family, then she came out of nowhere behind me. I thought maybe the voice was just some kids playing a joke, but I asked and Mattie said they had no kids. Of course, she also said Roberta had no kids. Maybe some of her tenants have kids. Maybe I'm just blowing this out of proportion."

"Slow down. You said you spoke to Mattie?"

"Yes, I had a very informative chat with our present landlady."

"And?" they said in unison.

"Stop doing that! It's creepy. We just talked about family, kids, that sort of thing."

"And then what? You heard a voice?"

"No, I heard the voice first. Wow, I'm starting to sound crazy even to myself. There's no telling what you guys think of me right now."

"We're just a little worried about you, that's all. What did the voice say?"

"Stop investigating my family."

"Well, there you go. It could have just been a disgruntled family member..."

"Maybe they're right. Maybe we shouldn't investigate any further. I don't need to know who my mother was. It's not like it's gonna do us any good and it may get us hurt or even killed. We don't know what these people are capable of."

"No. We've come too far to stop. We're already in this, whether we like it or not."

"Okay. But, you know this means we have to be much more careful about this. You are not to do anything unless at least one of us guys is with you. Okay?"

"Fine. Whatever. So, Jacob, have you filled Marshall in on tonight?"

"What about tonight?" Marshall asked

"Well, I figured we could do that together."

Chapter Twelve

That night, as soon as we figured that everyone else had gone to sleep, we began to prepare to go up to the attic. We had found miniature flashlights in an emergency backpack way in the back of the closet. We took these and our cell phones and put them in our pockets.

"I'd better bring this pocket knife just in case," said Marshall. "You never know what we'll need up there."

As we headed out of our room, we checked the hallway outside our door. When we had ascertained that the coast was clear, we crept past bedroom after bedroom until we made it to the dark stairwell.

"I'll go first," I volunteered. Marshall started to protest but I stopped him.

"I've already been up there. I can navigate a little better if I go first."

"We don't know what-or *who* is up there."

"I know exactly what's up there. It's just some boxes of mementos. You're not *scared*, are you?"

"No, I'm just concerned for *your* safety. You've already been threatened once today. Just, for my sanity, go between me and Jacob."

"Fine, but I don't think it's necessary."

As Marshall's foot slowly descended onto the first step, we all drew in a huge breath as the step began to creak. We listened for a moment to see if we had woken anyone up, but not a sound was heard. After a moment or two, we continued our ascent. We held our breath as each step we took seemed to sound through the whole inn.

Once at the top of the stairs, we silently rejoiced by letting the air that we had been holding in out of our lungs in a slow, quiet stream. We then shined our flashlights around the room to see what we were up against. *These boxes seem to have multiplied since I was up here before.*

Nevertheless, we all spread out to begin our search, though we weren't quite sure what we were looking for.

I began with a box near the window on the far side of the attic, figuring that we could all work our way to the middle of the room. I told the guys my plan and, to my surprise, they actually went along with it. It felt nice to be taken seriously as an equal to the men, but I told myself I mustn't let that go to my head.

In the first box, all I found were some old clothes from what looked like the seventies, and the second box and the third... It wasn't until I looked up that I saw that the rest of the boxes were full of newspapers. I began to look at them. The headlines read as follows: "Family Robbed Near Copake Lake," "String of Robberies Surrounds Copake Lake," "Copake Criminals Team Up," and "Copake Criminal Caught." But the one that really struck me was the last one I found. "Copake Criminal's Family Drives Care Into Lake, City Mourns."

"That's funny," I said out loud. "All of these articles seem to centered around some kind of robberies that took place near Copake Lake a long time ago.

"Yeah, I found some pictures taken on the lake," Marshall said.

"That's right near Aunt Beth. Maybe she'll know about these crimes."

"It's worth a shot. We should get back there anyway pretty soon. I'm sure Nathaniel would enjoy his own bed too." We continued to look for any other clues we might could use. As for me, I decided to read the articles one by one to see if there was any information we could use in them.

◆ ◆ ◆

After about an hour of skimming the articles, I finally found something interesting. "Look at this. It seems that Roberta was pregnant at the time of the crash. But what's really interesting is that this was a few months before you were born. That means, *if* Roberta was your mother, she could very well still be alive!"

Suddenly, Marshall jumped up, nearly shouting with excitement. "I found a birth certificate!" Jacob and I both tiptoed over to look at it. "Quick, what's your birth date?"

"May 17th 1986, why?"

"Listen to this. 'Born to Mr. Nathaniel Grey and Mrs. Roberta Hasting-Grey a baby boy' on your exact birth date!"

"Wow, I can't believe it! They were *married*! I didn't even know *that* much about my parents."

"Wait a minute. There's another one. To an unnamed father and Roberta Hasting a baby boy by the name of Henry Hasting. You have an older brother!"

"It appears our hostess is a fibber. She told me her sister never married *or* had children," I observed.

The next thing Marshall picked out of the box was a small leather-bound book that appeared to be a diary. *Roberta's* diary! We didn't know whether to look into its pages, no doubt filled with information that could shed more light on things, or whether to consider it an extreme invasion of privacy. But, considering that we had come so far already, we decided that we would skim through it.

As soon as we opened the book, it was as if we were instantly transported back in time to the world through the eyes of one young woman growing up in the eighties. We could almost hear the record players and see the roller skates swerving to and fro as if in an interpretive dance production. Back then, a girl's diary was all she had to do in her bedroom on a lazy day such as we had experienced earlier. All the entries were definitely that of a typical teenager. There were entries that entailed 'mom won't let me get a tattoo,' 'my first car,' and so on. Then, about halfway through the book were some very intriguing entries.

> *June 13, 1985*
> *Dear Diary,*
> *Today, I met the most amazing guy. We were out by the*
> *lake and the sun was just beginning to set. I was throwing*

a Frisbee with some friends and I admittedly threw it a bit hard, but from so far off, he caught my Frisbee! Then he asked if he could play with us. We agreed and we played until the lights came on up on the dock. But, as we were gathering our things, he came up and asked me to a movie! I'm so excited!

R

July 1, 1985
Dear Diary,
Nate and I are so perfect for each other! And he is so CHIVALROUS! He won't even let me open any doors or pay for my own meals with the money from my summer job down at the skating rink!

R

August 3, 1985
Dear Diary,
Nathaniel and I have decided to get married. I'm not sure how my parents are going to take it. Then again, they've been gone a lot lately. I wonder where they go?

R

August 17, 1985
Dear Diary
It's been almost two weeks since Nathaniel and I got married at the courthouse. The whole thing was a big secret from my folks. Then, afterward, we went straight to his side of the lake as Mr. and Mrs. Grey even though I had to keep my name for obvious reasons.

R

September 15, 1985

Dear Diary,

My brother has gone to jail! I can't believe this is hap-pening! My parents say that we have to go away and nev-er come back! What w3ill that do to my poor Nathaniel? They keep mentioning things like driving the car into the lake! I don't know what to do or think! I'm so scared! I need to get the love letters and put them in a safe place where no one will ever find them!

R

Chapter Thirteen

The next morning after reading those diary entries over again in the safety of our room, we stood there dumbfounded for what seemed like a few hours. Then, as if we were all of one mind, it occurred to all of us what we must do: return to Aunt Beth's and look for those letters. And we needed Nathaniel's help. If he could tell us which house she had lived in, that would narrow our search considerably.

As we began to pack for our trip back to the cabin, we heard a tap at the door.

"Who is it?" I called out.

"Open the door and find out," came a man's voice. We all looked at each other tentatively. Marshall went over and opened at the door. At the door stood a tall, rather banged-up man.

"Nathaniel!"

"Hello, kids! Well, aren't you going to invite me in?" Dumbfounded, Marshall stepped back and held the door open for Nathaniel to enter.

"Thank you, my boy."

"No problem. We are just glad to see you up and about."

"Well, I had very good doctors." He smiled as he sat on one of the unmade beds.

"*Doctors?*"

"Well, I can't forget the caring young people who pulled me out of that pile of trash, including my own son. What are the odds of that happening?"

Jacob, moving out of Nathaniel's line of sight, began waving his arms as if to say "Don't say a word."

He hadn't told Nathaniel that Roberta might still be alive! I stood completely still, astonished at this realization. *Oh no. This could throw the whole plane off course. He has to tell him! But, how? The man just got out of a hospital bed. Jacob's news will no doubt give him a heart attack and send him straight back into it!*

I come out of my reverie to see that Nathaniel was no longer in the room, only the two concerned faces of my brother and the man I love. "What happened to you?" Marshall queried, alarmed.

I took a few cleansing breaths to calm my nerves. "It just occurred to me that we have to tell Nathaniel that the love of his life could still be alive!"

"You're right," Jacob said absentmindedly. He then got up and began to pace the room. "Yeah, I've been thinking about that all night." My heart leapt out to him. Every fiber in my being just wanted to get up off this bed, cross the room, wrap my arms around him and give him a big hug, but I didn't. I sat there, patiently waiting to see what was to be done.

"Well, what are you going to do?" Marshall asked.

"What else *can* I do? I have to tell him." He began heading for the door.

"Whoa, you're going to go *now*?"

"No time like the present, right?"

"Aren't you worried about sending that poor man *back* into the hospital bed?" I interjected.

"I don't think it will be quite that dramatic. Most men aren't that sentimental. Well, I better get down there before I lose my nerve." He opened the door and walked out.

◆ ◆ ◆

It was a few hours before Jacob came back to the room. Marshall and I had been trying to keep our minds occupied with various activities. As soon as he came in, we jumped up from our respective activities in expectation of what Jacob had to say. "Well?" we both asked in unison.

"He took it well, I think," was all he had to say. Marshall and I both looked at him in disbelief.

"Well, what did he say?" I asked.

"Nothing."

"Oh, come on. You can tell us. You're among friends here," Marshall added.

"No, I mean he literally said nothing. He just sat there awestruck. I didn't know what to do. Finally, I just decided to leave him alone to process the information."

"I'm sorry, man. I know you must be worried."

"Aw, he'll come around. He just needs a while to process, that's all. It must be genetic. When *I* found out *myself*, if was hard enough to process. I can't imagine what it is like for him. He's probably been pining for her and grieving her loss for twenty-five years. And then, he finds out she might still be alive?"

"Well, I guess we'll give him the time to process. We certainly don't want to rush him in his current condition," I said.

"Right. The last thing we need is for him to collapse again. We'll just wait it out I guess. We still have to wait until the good doctor says it's okay for him to leave here."

"But, how is that going to work with us going to look for those letters that prove that Roberta is Jacob's mother?"

"I don't know. But I *do* know that staying here for at least another day would be best for Nathaniel."

"Yes, I suppose you might be right," I said "Don't worry. He'll come around. Now I wonder what Mattie has prepared for us for lunch."

◆ ◆ ◆

It took nearly twenty-four hours before we heard from Nathaniel again. We were sitting at the dining room table and he said "Pass the salt." It wasn't much but it was a start. We spent a few minutes trying to expand on it, to see if we could get him to say anything else all during lunch to no avail. It wasn't until we were alone in the room that he spoke to us in earnest.

"I met your mother so many years ago. It was a summer break that brought me to that lake. I was staying with your aunt and uncle for the summer. Some days, I would sit on the front porch and watch the sun set over the water. Other days, I would enjoy it out on the pier. It was such an evening when I met your mother. She was beautiful and the sweetest girl you'd ever meet. She was from the other side of the lake where the sun seemed to set right behind her house when I watched from that dock. It was a summer love that never truly ended for me. We sealed it in marriage one wonderful day and spent the rest of the evening out on the dock watching the waves dance in the reflection of the sun as if they were perfect dance partners. It was so romantic."

"Right. Yada, yada, yada and here I am today. Can we move on to what happened when her family found out?" Jacob cut in.

"Her parents never did like me. I didn't know what exactly it was, but I soon found out when one of them was convicted of several robberies in the neighborhood. Her father was so distraught, one day he just drove the car into the lake with the whole family in it and they all perished. Or at least I thought they had."

"That sounds like a terrible ordeal to have to go through!" I exclaimed. I couldn't imagine what I'd do if Jacob died.

"Yes, well, I wasn't the only one who mourned their passing. The whole town was out of sorts for months."

Suddenly, I remembered what we had been trying to convince him of.

"Well, what if I told you that I have a theory that Roberta may still be alive?"

"Oh, no. That could not be possible. I saw the obituaries in the paper the following Sunday," he said, completely assured of his accuracy.

"Yeah, I thought it was a long shot," Marshall said.

I frowned at him and continued. "Well, I happen to believe that it must be true. There is no other way to explain that Jacob is alive."

"You have a point. I never thought of it that way. It must be the case. My Roberta has to be alive."

"Whatever the case, we have a tip that there are some letters in the house she used to live in that prove she is my mother, some that she wrote to you."

"I never got any letters." Nathaniel cocked his head, puzzled.

"Well, perhaps they were letters that were written to you but never sent."

"Perhaps."

"Whatever the case, I would like to find them. Are you in?" Jacob asked as Nathaniel rubbed his scruffy chin in thought.

After a long pause, he said "Count me in."

♦ ♦ ♦

The next day, we all rose early in the morning and began packing our things and went downstairs to settle up with Mattie.

"Oh my, you're all leaving us so soon?"

"I'm afraid so," Marshall said. "We have to get back to our aunt's place. She's probably worried about us."

"Okay, if you must. I am sure that your aunt will be very pleased that you went back. I'm sure I'll be seeing you again real soon," she said with a polite smile as she took the money from Marshall. Then, we picked up our bags and headed out the door.

Once outside, we all loaded up the station wagon. It didn't take long, for we had only bought the necessities and one or two souvenirs for each of us, plus Marshall and I had each pitched in and gotten a get-well gift for Nathaniel. Plus, now we had extra space as Nathaniel was fully capable of sitting up front with Marshall, which he did, leaving Jacob and me to sit in the backseat.

I didn't know what to say to him, so I decided to get my phone out and play a game of solitaire. That held my attention for about five minutes until Marshall gave a low whistle. "Boy, all the drama's gone and nobody wants to talk anymore, huh?" He had never been able to handle silence for very long. So much so that he even had to have a fan on for noise to be able to sleep, no matter if it was summer or winter.

"I guess we are all just resting from the packing," I said.

"Oh, yeah. I forgot. It was ten whole minutes of packing," he mocked. But then, to my relief, he dropped the subject, opting for the radio instead.

Other than making one phone call to Aunt Beth to let her know we were coming back, we sat in silence for the rest of the trip.

♦ ♦ ♦

As soon as we turned into the driveway of Aunt Beth's cabin, we were greeted by the sight of an unfamiliar car parked in front of the house. Next, we saw a lanky blonde come out of the house and bound down the steps to meet us.

"Hi, I'm Christy Ann," she said, sticking her arm out to us once we'd gotten out of the car. "I'm just passing through on my way to the coastline and Beth offered to let me stay here for a few days on my way. And you must be the relatives that are staying with Beth and Joe for the summer."

"You're half right. I'm Marshall and this is my sister Samantha," he said, pointing back at me. "We are staying here. They live next door." He pointed at Nathaniel and Jacob, which made Jacob flinch. I gave him a questioning look, but got no answer, as Aunt Beth had emerged from the front door of the cabin and was waving at us to come in. But, as soon as we got close, Aunt Beth gasped and ran into the house yelling "Joe!"

Chapter Fourteen

As soon as we all had walked in the door, Marshall, Jacob, Nathaniel and I went straight to the room that Marshall and I shared.

"Now, everyone," instructed Marshall, "I don't think it's a good idea to tell anyone what we have experienced. Obviously, judging by her reaction, she is going to ask how we know Nathaniel. But, the whole hospital part and all that about the poison, let's just keep that to ourselves. I believe there might still be lives at stake if anything should get out to the wrong people." We all nodded in shaky agreement.

During dinner that night, we took turns telling Aunt Beth and Uncle Joe about how we knew Nathaniel. Well, some of it anyway. It was difficult, but we left out all the dangerous bits.

"You thought Nathaniel was snooping around in the neighboring house?" she asked. We all looked around at each other.

"I guess so," I said. "I thought he might've been the gardener or something after we spoke to him, though. It took until Jacob said that he was his son that we put it together that he lived there."

Suddenly, a light bulb came on in my head. *But, when he was in the hospital, we had looked in that very same house for his papers! That is his house! I wonder if it's the same house he'd lived in so long ago.* I couldn't believe it. Was he living there? Was Jacob living there with him? With all these thoughts swimming through my head, I had not been listening to the conversation, so I was caught off-guard when suddenly I noticed that all eyes around the table were on me.

"I'm sorry. Can you repeat the question?" I asked, shaking my head as if all the other thoughts would just shake off.

"I asked how you liked staying at Catherine's house?" I looked from Aunt Beth to Marshall, who gave me a quick wink.

"Oh, yeah. It was great." *How did Catherine get dragged into all of this again?*

The rest of the evening, I pretty much kept to myself. As soon as dinner was over, I went straight to the bedroom and started reading the book that I had borrowed from Jillian until about ten o'clock, at which time Marshall came in and lay on his bed. "So, this is where you disappeared to."

"Yeah, I just didn't feel like talking. I was afraid I would give something away."

"Ah. Totally understandable. Well, I think we've had a pretty eventful day, don't you?"

"Definitely."

"So, why don't we hit the hay already, huh?"

"You don't have to tell me twice."

"Oh. By the way, I've told the guys that we are going to search Roberta's house tomorrow. We are all going to disappear from this house one by one in the morning and meet up at the pier, where Nathaniel will then tell us which house we need to search before we get ourselves arrested casing the wrong house. If we're at the right house, no one should bother us. According to Nathaniel, no one has lived in the house since the 'incident' that supposedly killed the Hastings."

"Sounds like you have it all figured out," I yawned. "Good night."

♦ ♦ ♦

When we rose in the morning, it was very early. The sun had not yet come up and even the crickets were still asleep it seemed. We dressed in light layers to accommodate any change in the weather. We crept stealthily through the living room to the sliding glass door. Marshall looked back at me, making a shushing signal. I glared at the back of his head as he slowly began to unlatch the door. Suddenly, reflected in the glass, we saw that a light was turned on. We struggled to get the door open as quickly as we possibly could and made it out in the nick of time and ran smack into Catherine, who was just about to knock on the door.

"Hey, guys. What's the big hurry?"

"Well, um," I stammered, "we actually have to meet at the dock for a big project."

"A big project? Can I help?"

We were hesitant at first but we didn't have time to argue and we figured we could use the extra hands if we were going to find the letters today. We agreed and proceeded to run across the yard and toward Nathaniel's dock, where we were to meet Jacob and him.

Once we made it to the dock the others were already there waiting for us. "So, what's the plan, Captain?" Nathaniel asked, looking at Marshall.

"First of all, we picked up an extra helper. So, I figured we could probably find the letters if we have the whole day. Right now, we need you to tell us where the house is."

"I'll do better than that. I'll take you right to it."

"Even better."

◆ ◆ ◆

We made it to the house in less than twenty minutes on foot. You could tell from the road that no one had lived in it for quite some time. There in front of us barely stood a small brick house with the door hanging precariously on one of its hinges. We went a little closer. There were animal food and water bowls that had long been empty on the small covered porch. Beside that were two wicker chairs that had definitely seen better days. I moved toward the door frame. The house was very simple inside. It looked as though all the rooms were combined into one room. There was a couch and TV in one corner and a washing machine behind the couch. In the other corner was a mattress on which I suppose the whole family had slept. The kitchen consisted of a hotplate, a toaster, a wood-burning stove and a small refrigerator. The only other room was a bathroom. The other door led to the back of the property. The whole place seemed to be pretty neat and tidy, though. It was almost as if the family had tidied up before they left on their inauspicious journey. *This shouldn't take long at all.*

We spread out and each took a corner of the room. We decided that it was safe to assume she hadn't hidden the letters in the bathroom. We checked couch cushions, under everything, even trying to kick up the floor boards but to no avail. It took us about an hour to check the whole room, but we decided to check again, this time switching locations to get different perspectives on everything. We checked every cabinet and cranny. We found nary a single letter, nor postcard, not even any junk mail lying around. So, we moved on to the next stop: The backyard.

As we opened the back door, it gave a loud squeak, making each of us cringe with fright as if the owners of the house would show up and do who knows what to us. Then, we all remembered that nobody had been here for twenty-five years and relaxed. We all smiled at ourselves for getting scared and continued on our course. The backyard smelled awful and was full of tall weeds. They were so tall, we could barely see the roof of an old work shed over them. We all looked around at one another wondering what we should do.

"Let's check out that shed," Marshall instructed. We all nodded. I was very glad we had him to lead us. I certainly would not have wanted to do it. We made our way through the tall grass toward the barn, almost making a swimming motion to get through the massive amounts of weeds. We worked through the barn the same way we had done the house, but nothing was found. We all looked around hopelessly, wondering where she could have hidden the letters that we had not already checked.

"Oh!" Nathaniel shouted. "I nearly forgot!" He began to run toward the house. We all looked around at one another, shrugged and followed him through the back door. When we had caught up to him, he was struggling to move the mattress. Before we even had time to be confused, we all began to help him lift the mattress until we saw what he was trying to get to: A small door in the floor. Our next issue became apparent, though, when we realized that the latch to the trapdoor was broken in a way that would make it very difficult to open. Thankfully, I remembered seeing a crow bar out in the old shed. I had picked it up in case any situation that may arise. I gave it to Jacob, who then proceeded to work on wedging it between the door and the floor. I marveled at the bulging muscles in his arm as he worked on the door, wishing they would hold me again one day. Then, I caught Marshall looking at me with a warning expression on his face. When Jacob finally got the door open, there was a loud cracking noise and a cloud of dust that had all our eyes watering.

Down in the hole was a wooden staircase that was definitely very old and dilapidated.

Marshall checked the first step. "Steady as a fifty-year-old stair should be, I suppose."

"I'll go first," said Nathaniel, who then took a flashlight out of a pre-pared bag that he had brought for our little expedition. He shined the flashlight on the first two steps, then on the wall as he fumbled for a light switch. When he had found the switch, the whole room was illuminated in a fluorescent light. We all stood at the top of the stairs looking around at the immense room in front of us.

"This basement has to be bigger than the actual house!" Catherine remarked.

"Well, this is where the family stored all there extra stuff," Nathaniel answered. In the room were so many things, they were stacked up to the ceiling in some places. In one of the corners was an old snake skin that I was sure had been there for ages. In another corner was a cobweb high up on the ceiling.

"I'll take this corner," I said, steering myself away from the offending corners. We all got to work promptly, for we knew what a project this would be.

I searched in box after box and crate after crate, finding all the afore-mentioned junk mail and a few letters from members of the family to one another. I tossed these aside and kept digging. Finally, I found some-thing promising. It was a manila envelope full of smaller envelopes. "I found something!"

That's when we heard them. Three ominous slow claps that came from the top of the stairs. "I'm so glad you found my sister's letters," said a very recognizable voice. Then, from the stairs descended Mattie and Clive, guns in hand. We had nowhere to go and nothing we could do but hold up our hands in defeat.

"I assume you've all met Clive, *my brother.*" *Brother! That makes so much sense now. They've been living incognito as husband and wife all this time under the pretense of being simply inn owners!*

"Tie them up," she ordered. Clive obediently followed direction. She started toward me. "You see, I really don't want to have to do this, but it's really not up to me."

"Yes it is. You don't have to do anything you don't want to do," Marshall said through gritted teeth as Clive tightened the frayed rope around his wrists.

"You just don't see the big picture, do you? Well, let me explain it to you. There is a chance that there is some very serious and compromising information in this envelop that, if it lands into the wrong hands, could lead to a lot of trouble. My sister always *was* the sentimental type." Mattie said the last few words as if it left a bad taste in her mouth. "Now, the whole question is which one of you I kill first. Or whether to use a gun or to play around with it a little. Well, there *are* four of you. Plenty to play around with a little." Suddenly, we heard two distinct thuds from above. "What is that? Go check it out. I'll look at the letters."

"But, the hostages-"

"They aren't going anywhere. Just go on up and take a look." She looked from Clive to us. "Now, for these letters," she said as she sat at the table in one of the corners. "Oh, what mushy love letters. You two must have been very much in love. Blech! In my opinion, no one understands love.

"And you do?" I asked from my corner of the room(the one with the cobweb in it).

"Dear, didn't you hear what I said? No one, myself included, understands love. That is the bottom line. Romeo and Juliet has never happened in real life. There are not always happy endings. Especially not for the five of you saps. I had better go check on Clive. Just to make sure he hasn't botched the whole plan already." Once she was gone, I could tell that every one of our heads were reeling as to how to get out of this situation.

"Any ideas?" Jacob, who was tied to a large clay planter right next to me, directed his question to Marshall on the other side of the room.

"Oh! I just remembered that I have a pocket knife in my pocket. If I could just... Aha, got it." He had had his hands tied behind his back, and the knife was in his back pocket, easy to reach. I assumed that he got it open and was working on getting his restraints cut, though I was facing the opposite direction.

"Got it. Who's next?" He had barely begun to cut the rope from off Nathaniel's wrists when we heard Mattie's feet coming down the stairs. He quickly assumed his position as she made her way down.

"Hmmm, suspicious that you haven't moved an inch since I've been gone. Surely, in a normal situation, you'd be trying to get out. I don't suppose you're dumb enough for that, huh?" She walked over to the table with the letters and the gun on it. "Nobody stole my gun. Just brilliant of you, I say," she mocked. "Well, I had better put it to use now that I've put the idea in your heads." She now had the gun pointed at Marshall's head. He closed his eyes.

"You know, Clive and I heard all your little conversations in the inn. We knew all about everything. I knew I had recognized your friend here." She waved the gun over toward Nathaniel and back to Marshall. "But, I just could not figure out from where until you all were in my attic. I couldn't bust you right then either."

Just then, we heard two more sets of footsteps coming down the stairs of the basement. We knew one of them had to be Clive, but who was the second? Could it be Roberta? Or another sibling of theirs? We were soon to find out for the steps finally came down into the basement. We watched horrified as Clive came down with an additional hostage: Aunt Beth!

"Beth! No! What are you doing here?"

"I knew you kids were in trouble the moment I saw Nathaniel," she said as she was pushed down to a seated position on the floor.

"Quiet!" cried Mattie. "Now what are we gonna do with all six of your bodies?"

Suddenly, we heard another voice come as if out of nowhere. "Let them go, Aunt Mattie!"

"Well, if it isn't the prodigal nephew. Have you really come to rescue your brother and all that sentimental mumbo-jumbo?" Mattie asked. *Brother? Who is that?*

"You bet. Come on, Mattie Ann, you know that I know far more than they do. You'll get your biggest pest out of the way and get a lot less jail time for killing one person than you would six." The figure came down the stairs halfway just to where you could see a silhouette. *The man from the morgue!* I nudged Jacob behind me to look at what I was seeing and could see his eyes widen as he realized who it was, then a look of confusion came onto his face as if to say *my brother?* I moved my hand so that it was on top of his and threw an apologetic look over in his direction. He held on tight for a moment, then relaxed.

"Hmmmmm. Alright, you got a deal. I'm getting tired of these love-birds and their PDA anyway. Come help me untie them."

"Gladly," he said as he came out of the shadows. There stood a tall, well-built, blonde-haired, green-eyed man that, other than a few differences, looked just like Jacob.

"Wow," I said. I felt Jacob cringe behind me. Marshall and the rest gasped.

"Henry, I would like you to meet your half-brother, Jacob, said Aunt Mattie as she untied him and helped him to his feet. Jacob breathed a sigh of relief at being loosed from the ropes and looked at his brother, who was busy untying Catherine. When he finished, he held out his hand to Jacob. After shaking hands, they each began helping the rest of us. As soon as I was free, I threw my arms around Jacob and hugged him for about half a minute. Once everyone was free and we began to make our exit, Henry held out his hand to me.

"Pleasure to see you again," he said, smiling asa he slipped another piece of paper into my hand. It seemed strange to me that he wasn't even worried about what was soon to happen to him.

◆ ◆ ◆

"We've got to get him out of there," said Jacob as soon as we were out of the house.

"I agree," said Marshall. "Everybody in?

"I'm in," I said.

"Me too," Catherine said.

"If you're all in, count me in too," said Aunt Beth.

"So, what's the plan?" asked Nathaniel.

"Well, I have some information Henry slipped into my hand as we were leaving that might be helpful."

"What does it say?"

Fight fire with fire.

Chapter Fifteen

"What is that supposed to mean?" Marshall asked.

"Well, the thing that comes to mind right away is to take that literally and light the place up," Nathaniel said.

"I don't think that's really what it means," I said, leery of the idea.

"Alright, alright. I have a plan," Marshall said. "First off, we need to find some dirt on Mattie. No, wait. That won't work in the time we need it to," he muttered to himself. "Aha, we have to get our own hostage. That's got to be what it means…"

"And how do you suppose we do that?" Catherine folded her arms.

"We have to get Clive alone."

◆ ◆ ◆

A few moments later, the plane was already made, the trap set, and we were heading for the front door of the old house once again. This time, we didn't hesitate or knock on the door. We opened the door and walked straight in. Then, Marshall started jumping up and down. Soon, we could hear Clive's clumsy footsteps coming up the stairs. We quickly shuffled around to our places. Once we had all found our places, all that was left to do was wait.

As soon as I was in place, I could hear Clive's grumblings as he walked up the stairs. When I saw the trapdoor to the basement lift halfway, I readied myself to do my part of the plan. Then, the trapdoor was opened fully and Clive skeptically emerged from the stairwell. Once he was all the way out, I quickly released the mattress behind which I had been hiding, which fell onto the basement door, covering the opening. Nathaniel and Jacob then stepped in front of the doors so there was no way out. Catherine and Beth came out of hiding and, before he even knew what hit him, Catherine threw a rope around him and cinched it tight.

"Okay, so this is how this is going to go," Marshall began. "You are not going to scream because we are not going to hurt you. We just want some information."

"You can try, but you won't get anything out of me," Clive sneered.

"Oh, in that case, I have a better idea. Gag him and bind his feet. We wouldn't want him calling out or running off now, would we?" Catherine obeyed orders shakily.

"Next we are going to play a little game. Have you ever heard of the game 'Red Rover, Red Rover'?" Clive shook his head fearfully. "Lift the mattress. I'm going down." I obeyed and he went down the stairs to the basement. We waited in silence.

When Marshall finally came up, he was not alone. There in his somewhat worse-for-wear condition was Henry, alive and in the flesh.

"How'd you do it?" asked Jacob with his rehearsed excitement.

"It was easy. I just told her we had her brother and she offered a trade just like that. In fact, it was a little *too* easy."

Suddenly, seemingly from out of nowhere, a horseshoe flew across the room and buzzed past Marshall's ear. "You didn't really think I was gonna let you get away that easy, did you?" Mattie asked from the top of the stairs.

Next thing we knew, we were running. We ran as fast and as far as we could until we had to look back to see where Mattie was. She was climbing into an old truck that looked like it had been parked there for as long as the house had been abandoned. Nevertheless, it started, though it took a few turns of the key. We ran like mad until we each decided to climb a very leafy tree for cover and still be able to watch her.

"Why is she so angry?" I asked Marshall.

"Because I have this," he said as he reached into his pocket and pulled out a white envelope. "It's the letter she had been looking at when I went down there. Then, when she was untying Henry, she had no one to watch me or the letters, so I took it. Okay, she's driven far enough past us. It's safe to go down now."

We made our way down the trees with extreme caution in case she doubled back looking for us, but we saw where she was heading soon. When we made it out of the wooded area, the truck was half-sunk in the water and her door was open. She'd fallen head first into the bank trying to get away. Before we knew what was happening, we were surrounded by a swarm of police patrol cars, sirens blaring. Mattie was lifted out of the muddy water and promptly handcuffed and led to one of the patrol cars.

One of the officers walked over to us. "We got a call for a disturbance in the neighborhood, but I recognized the woman we just arrested right away. I had proof that she was still alive and I've been trying to nab her for years and you kids single-handedly brought her down at once."

"Well, what have you been trying to bring her in for?"

"Embezzlement, fraud, money laundering, you name it."

"Well, I'm glad things worked out. By the way," Marshall said, as he pulled out the envelope. "Here's a few more crimes to add to the list." He handed the folded letter to the officer. On the outside were the words, "To My Darling, Nathaniel." The officer opened it up and read the contents.

> *Dear Nathaniel,*
>
> *I'm so sorry I have not the time to give you this letter before I go. Just know that I will always love you and cherish the few short months that we had together.*
>
> *My love, there is something that I need to tell you. I know that my family is the culprit behind the Copake crimes. Please take this letter to the police when I am gone. Let them know that we are in hiding and not dead. I am so ashamed that I could not tell you to your beautiful face. Know that I am forever yours,*
>
> *R*

As soon as I finished reading the letter over the officer's shoulder, I looked up to see Uncle Joe coming over the top of the hill. I made my way over to him.

"I had an idea you kids might be in some kind of trouble. I sent your aunt to follow you and when she reported back where you were, I immediately called the police, knowing that could not lead to anything good." He wrapped his arms around me in a big hug. "I'm glad that you are safe."

"Do you mind if I asked you about what you've been working on in the shed?"

"Not at all. It's time somebody knew. Your aunt and I have an anniversary coming up and I've been working on a small gift."

"Small? It's taken up half your time and the whole shed for the past few weeks."

"Okay, so it's slightly bigger than small," he laughed and kissed me on the top of my head. "Come on, let's go get some hot cocoa."

"Hold on. There is one more thing I need to do," I said as I released him and began to make my way over to make my way over to Jacob.

"You know, I know that you are right that I am not alone," I said to him.

"Well, I am glad that you see all the loving people around you. Family is something that I have recently learned to appreciate and I definitely want to make sure what you have in your big crazy family."

"Okay, I understand." With that off his chest, he began to retreat to his house... Wait a minute. "Hey!" I called out. "Where did you go that one day I didn't see your truck here? And why wouldn't Nathaniel be upset about that?"

"Because I don't live with him," he said, when I had caught up with him. "I have an apartment in Hillsdale. It must seem like I'm here a lot for not living with him, but wouldn't you do the same?"

"Yes. You are right."

He nodded, then turned around and walked away. As for me, I walked about aimlessly, trying to make sense of what all I had learned until I ended up walking out toward our dock where everything was calm and I cried and cried for so long that tears seemed to flow as a river from my eyes. I cried for everything that had happened and all the lives that were changed and the fact of my possibly unrequited love. I must have been there for half an hour before I heard footsteps walking slowly up the dock. Suddenly a warm fluffy coat surrounded me with its welcome comfort.

◆ ◆ ◆

His voice broke the silence. "Where's Marshall?"

"Oh, he's probably still with the police or something." I shook my head then, looking at him, I asked "What are you doing here? You should be with Nathaniel and Henry."

"Oh, they're fine without me. I actually wanted to talk to Marshall."

"Oh," I said, lowering my eyes to the water below my feet. Sitting right next to me now, he brought his hand up and tenderly nudged my head up by the chin so that our eyes met. As his body supported mine on the old dock and his arms were around me, my heart thudded and pitter-pattered with hop.

"There's one thing in particular that I wanted to speak with him about."

"Oh?" I asked. One part of me was terrified of what he was going to say next, but another part of me was dying to know what it was. To my utter amazement, he reached inside his jacket that was still draped around me, and pulled out a quite familiar little black box with the same white water lily design on top.

"I know I was supposed to ask your parents about this first, but I considered that Marshall was the closest thing you had right now and that he's your best friend and I figured that was a start."

I took the box and opened it. *Yep, the same ring*, I thought. "I can't believe you've kept this all this time." I looked at him. He was looking at me as if his life depended on the smile on my face. He took the little box from my hand, got up and knelt on one knee, taking the infamous proposal position.

Blushing, I stood up and said "I will marry you on one condition."

He looked completely thrilled and desperately expectant. "You name it, it's yours. I've got Saturn's rings on back order," he said.

"No, I just need the one ring for now. My condition is that you never take no for an answer again."

Relieved and ecstatic, he slipped the diamond ring on my left hand, got up, picked me up and proceeded to carry me back toward the cabin.

"Uh, Jake?" I said.

"Yes, dear?"

"Correct me if I'm wrong, but isn't this the sort of thing you do after the wedding?"

"I don't know what you're talking about," he said with a mischievous grin. All of a sudden, he spun around and headed straight toward the end of the dock. Before I would even shout, we were in the water with a huge splash.

Once I shook the water from my ears, I said "You know, this seems oddly familiar."

And, as do all good stories, this one ends with a kiss.

THE END

Epilogue

It's been two weeks since Jacob popped the question and I couldn't be more excited. You know, aside from the cold we both caught from our little swim that day.

As I packed up my things from Aunt Beth's a few days after my fever broke, I couldn't help but glance at my engagement ring every few minutes. The way it glistened in the sunlight was enough to make me swoon as I shoved pile after pile of sweaters into my various suitcases.

Suddenly, a knock on the door frame startles me. "Staring at your ring again?" Marshall enters the room with a big smile.

"Yes, and I have yet to find a single imperfection," I said, perkily.

"Oh, so you're a diamond expert now? I think you're just biased."

"Maybe," I conceded. "So, do you and Catherine have any special plans for tonight?"

"Who? Oh, you mean my *girlfriend!*" he said. "I just like to say it."

"Now, who's on cloud nine?" I joked.

"Anyway, I thought the whole group of us could go to the bagel place and just hang out tonight. Sort of a farewell-for-now thing."

"Sounds perfect to me."

Now, enjoy an excerpt from my next book, Mother of the Groom.

C h a p t e r   O n e

Samantha

"All done here," my brother Marshall updates as he moved the last suit-case from our station wagon to the beautiful 8-acre piece of land that my family lived on. "I'm going to go call Catherine and let her know we made it home safely."

You see, my brother and I had spent the last couple of months at my Aunt Beth's house all the way across the country. But I was glad to be home to see my family, even though it meant leaving behind my fiancé, Jacob, and my new friend and Marshall's girlfriend, Catherine. Yes, it seems the distance is going to be hard on us all. We had gotten quite used to seeing each other nearly every day. But, we all promised to e-mail and call one another at least most days.

The question was, though, when I was going to tell my family that I was engaged, and to the very man whose marriage proposal I had re-fused three years earlier. Yes, this was definitely a subject that needed to be broached carefully. At one point during the two-day drive home, I spoke to Marshall, my older brother who had come with me to New York, about the situation.

I remember I had just woken up from a short nap when my brother spoke first.

"I can't wait to tell the family all about our trip. What do you think?"

"Well, just hold on to some of those details until I tell them about Jacob," I said.

"Oh yeah. When do you think that will be, by the way?"

"I'll probably wait until I get settled back into being at home and what not."

Marshall gave me a skeptical look, then returned his gaze back to the road. "Just don't wait too long. You don't want to risk hurting their feelings."

"I'll know when the time is right," I guaranteed, thinking to myself that perhaps waiting until the day of the wedding would save us a long, agonizing discussion. Or it could ruin the most important day of my life.

Coming out of my reflection as I was headed toward the house from the station wagon, I caught sight of something I had left on the dashboard. It was the book that I had borrowed from my little sister, Jillian, for the trip. I opened the door, retrieved it and stuffed it into my purse along with my engagement ring.

Now, all tucked into my room, I made sure the door was closed and decided to give Jacob a call. I pull my phone out of my purse and hit speed-dial. He picked it up on the first ring.

"Well, it's about time you called," he chided. But, before I could defend myself, he continued. "Did you get home yet?"

"Yes, and we are all unpacked, at least from the car," I said. "Now, all I have to do is put it all away. My room is a mess right now. When Colleen gets home, she is going to freak out. By the way, speaking of Colleen, what would you think about me making her maid-of-honor?"

"Uh, that's up to you. I mean, she *is* your sister. Who else did you have in mind?"

"Well, there is Catherine, but technically, I've hardly known her more than a month."

"Good grief. Don't you have any friends down there?"

"Of course I do. I've lived here my whole life. Which brings me to another wedding-related topic: I can't believe we have to choose between Texas and New York for the ceremony. What's your vote?"

"I'll have to get back to you on that. My dad and Henry are supposed to be coming over in a little while. Did I tell you I have been visiting with him a lot lately?"

"No, you hadn't, but that's great to hear! I'm so glad you two are getting to know each other a little better considering he is your half-brother and all."

You see, Jacob had just met his half-brother about three weeks ago, so they were still in the getting—to—know—each—other phase of their relationship. But, they definitely were off to a great start because their first encounter was of a somewhat rocky nature. To make a long story short, their family has a lot of old baggage.

"My thoughts exactly. Well, I have to go. I love you and I'm glad you're home safely. I'll call you tomorrow."

"Love you too. Bye."

As I hang up the phone, my younger sister, Colleen swung open the door to the room we share.

"What happened here? It looks like a tornado has been through the place."

"Hello, Colleen. It's nice to see you too. I'm doing great. Thanks for asking," I said as if I were offended by her greeting.

"Hi, Sam," she said. "How was New York?"

"Pretty good. Aunt Beth and Uncle Joe were very hospitable. We made some new friends from up there."

"Oh, that's nice. I'm glad to hear that you weren't totally bored up there without me," she joked.

"Well, it was hard at first, but we got through it somehow," I fired back.

"Haha. Oh, I just remembered I told Mom that I would help her with something," she said as she hopped off of the bed.

"I'll go with you. I haven't seen Mom yet." I tore myself away from the bed and got the book out of my purse to give back to Jillian. She wasn't home from school yet, so I just leaned into her room and tossed it onto her bed.

"There's my long—lost daughter!" my mother shouted from the other end of the hall.

"Hi, Mom," I said as I closed the gap between us and wrapped her in an affectionate embrace.

"Hello, dear. Do you have any news from your aunt and uncle? Are they doing well?"

"They're great. In fact, just before we left, Uncle Joe gave Aunt Beth this really elaborate anniversary gift. It was a big spectacle, with an unveiling and everything."

"Well, what was the gift?" my mother asked.

"It was a handmade jewelry box. You should have seen it. This thing was about the size of a mini-fridge!"

"Wow, that's really impressive. Did your uncle make it all by himself or did he have help?"

"He had some associate from before he retired come over and help occasionally. I think his name was Daniel or something like that."

"Hmmm, interesting. Well, it sounds like my sister married well after all. Well, I'd better go figure out what I'm going to cook for dinner."

◆ ◆ ◆

That night at dinner, I enjoyed being with my big, loud family. My six siblings and I all shared experiences of the past few weeks. After dinner, my dad and the boys all adjourned to the living room to watch TV, while the girls remained in the dining room to clean up the kitchen and chat.

"So, Sam tells me that she made some new friends while she was up there in New York," Colleen spat out. I began to think about how I was going to skirt around this subject without revealing too much.

"Well, you know, there was this really nice waitress," I said carefully, then changed the subject, hoping no one would notice. "So, what happened here while I was gone? Anything new?"

"No, it was pretty much the same old story. Oh, except the neighbors got a new dog from a shelter in the city. I noticed him when I went walking down the road one evening. Very friendly. Hardly barked at me at all. I think he's a terrier of some sort."

"Well, that's cool I guess," I said. I'd dodged the bullet. That is, until Colleen opened her big mouth again.

"So, did you meet anybody *else*? You know, of the *romantic* sort?" *Groan!* How was I going to handle this subject?

"Yes, that makes a lot of sense. Finding a guy under the watchful eye of our aunt and uncle," I said sarcastically.

"You never know. It could happen..." she said, but then the subject was dropped as we all just went our separate ways to wind down from the day.

Made in the USA
Middletown, DE
20 December 2022

16879342R00080